SCOTTISH
SHORT STORIES

A Los Angeles swimming pool attendant in love with his pools; a British soldier turned rapist, patrolling the streets of Northern Ireland; the Peeping Tom of a most respectable London neighbourhood; an unemployed father killing time in a Glasgow housing estate; a young girl who awaits release from a mental hospital; an artist near the end of his working life; an elderly schoolteacher obsessed with the First World War; a witch seeking revenge on a laird for the seduction of her daughter: these are among the characters who appear in *Scottish Short Stories 1983*.

As in the previous ten volumes in this series published jointly by William Collins and the Scottish Arts Council, there is a remarkable diversity here which reflects, Joan Lingard writes in her Preface, the Scots' 'tendency to pull in different directions'. At a time when the short story form is enjoying new popularity, this year's Scottish collection is as stylish and entertaining as ever.

SCOTTISH
SHORT STORIES
1983

Preface by Joan Lingard

COLLINS
Grafton Street, London
1983

William Collins Sons & Co Ltd
London · Glasgow · Sydney · Auckland
Toronto · Johannesburg

First published in 1983

The publisher acknowledges the financial assistance of the Scottish Arts Council in the publication of this volume.

ISBN 0 00 222708/8

Photoset in Imprint
Made and printed in Great Britain by
William Collins Sons & Co Ltd Glasgow

CONTENTS

PREFACE

There is no school of Scottish short story writing; indeed, there is no school of Scottish writing, of any kind. The Scots are a race of individuals, perhaps even at times too much so, with a strong tendency to pull in different directions. But when it comes to the writing of short stories then this is a trait to be welcomed.

In this, the eleventh volume of the series, gathered together are sixteen stories by a diverse collection of people who are either Scottish by birth or parentage or else resident in Scotland. Each one speaks with a unique voice. The settings range from the Orcadian coast to a Glasgow housing scheme, from the streets of West Belfast to a swimming pool in Los Angeles to a village in the Alps. Themes explored include illusion and reality, wife-battering, role reversal, the survival instinct, and of course love, in its many different forms.

We have the traditional tale well told by Eona Macnicol, the portrait of a soldier turned rapist most convincingly built up by Carl MacDougall, a cameo of suburban life subtly revealed by Giles Gordon. In *The Care and Attention of Swimming Pools*, one of the most original stories in the collection, William Boyd takes us into the mind and heart of a swimming pool attendant who is in love with his pool. And in *Greater Love* we have a thoughtful, moving story from Iain Crichton Smith about a schoolteacher obsessed by the horror of the First World War and his need to convey it to the boys in his charge in the hope of saving them from suffering as he did. We have too fine contributions from such well-known writers as George Mackay Brown and Elspeth Davie.

This year's panel, James Campbell, Hilary Davies and myself, makes no apology for introducing only one writer – Stephanie Markman – who could be claimed as relatively new. We would have been happy to include a greater number of less well-known names, but it has never been the policy of the series to put novelty before quality. We chose the best, in our joint opinion, of what was offered.

The life of a short story is usually short. Magazines – the few that do exist – tend to be read and discarded, and radio is transitory. One of the attractions of these volumes is that they provide a place where the work of Scotland's short story writers can be gathered together and preserved. Looking back over the years, one sees what a valuable collection has been built up.

When the series was first launched by the Scottish Arts Council and Collins in 1973, Neil Paterson wrote in his preface, 'This book is a beginning.' It was a beginning that was well worth making.

JOAN LINGARD

THE CARE
AND ATTENTION OF
SWIMMING POOLS

William Boyd

Listen to this. Read it to yourself. Out Loud. Read it slow and think about it.

> A swimming pool is like a child,
> Leave it alone and it will surely run wild.

Who said that? Answer. Me. I did.

WINTERING

'Can I swim?' says Noelle-Joy. 'It's a fantastic pool.'

Much as I would like to see her jugs in a swimsuit I have to say no.

'Aw. Pretty please? Why not?'

'I'm afraid the pool is wintering.'

Noelle-Joy squints sceptically up at the clear blue sky. There's not even any smog today. She exposes the palms of her hands to the sun's powerful rays.

'But it's *hot*, man. Anyways, we don't get no winter in LA,' she argues.

Patiently I explain that, four seasons or no, every pool has to winter. A period of rest. What you might call a pool-sabbath. I've lowered the water level below the skimmers, surchlorinated, and washed out my cartridge filter. A pool, as I explain several times a day to my clients, is not just a hole in the ground filled with water. Wintering removes constant wear and tear, rests the incessantly churning pump machinery, allows essential repairs and maintenance, permits cleansing of the canals, filter system and heating units. You can't do all that if you're splashing around in the goddam thing. Most people realize I'm talking sense.

We walk around my pool. It's small but it's got everything. No-Skid surrounds, terrace lights, skimmers, springboard, all-weather poolside furniture, and a bamboo cocktail bar plus hibachi. I've got to admit it looks kind of peculiar stuck in my little back yard. (In this part of the city it's the only private pool for seventeen blocks.) But so what! I busted my balls for that little baby. I got me a new vacuum sweep last month. I'm aiming for a sand filter now, to replace my old cartridge model.

I stand proudly behind the bar and pour Noelle-Joy a drink. She's wearing a yellow halter neck and tight purple shorts. Maybe if she was a little thinner they'd look a bit better on her . . . I don't know. If you got it, flaunt it, I guess. Her legs are kind of short and her thighs have got that strange rumpled look. She stacks her red hair high on top of her head to compensate. She lights a Kool, sips her drink, sighs and hugs herself. Then she sees my hibachi and screams. I drop my cocktail shaker.

'My God! A hibachi. Permanent as well. Hey, can we bar-b-q? Please? Don't tell me that's wintering too.'

I ignore her sarcasm. 'Sure,' I say, picking up ice cubes. 'Come by tomorrow.'

I work for AA1 Pools (Maintenance) Inc. We've also been ABC Pools and Aardvark Pools. I tell my boss Sol Yorty that we should call ourselves something like Azure Dreams, Paradise Pools, Still Waters – that kind of name.

Yorty laughs and says it's better to be at the head of the line in Yellow Pages than sitting on our butts, poor, with some wise-ass, no-account trademark. The man has no pride in his work. If I wasn't up to my ears in hock to him I'd quit and set up on my own. TROPICAL LAGOONS, BLUE DIAMOND POOLS . . . I haven't settled on a name yet. The name is important.

GREEN WATER

Down Glendale Boulevard, Hollywood Freeway, on to Santa Monica Freeway. Got the ocean coming up. Left into Brentwood. Client lives off Mandeville Canyon. My God, the houses in Brentwood. The *pools* in Brentwood. You've never seen swimming pools like them. All sizes, all shapes, all eras. But nobody looks after them. I tell you, if pools were animate, Brentwood would be a national scandal.

The old Dodge van stalls on the turn up into the driveway. Yorty's got to get a new van soon, for Christ's sake. I leave it there.

The house stands at the top of a green ramp of lawn behind a thick laurel hedge. It's a big house, Spanish colonial revival style with half timbered English Tudor extension. A hispanic manservant takes me down to the pool. 'You wait here,' he says. Greaser. I don't like his tone. One thing I've noticed about this job, people think a pool cleaner is lower than a snake's belly. They look right through you. I was cleaning a pool up on Palos Verdes once. This couple started balling right in front of me. No kidding.

The pool. Thirty yards by fifteen. Grecian pillared pool house and changing rooms. Marble topped bar. Planted round with oleanders. I feel the usual sob build up in my throat. It's quiet. There's a small breeze

11

blowing. I dip my hand in the water and shake it around some. The sun starts dancing on the ripples, wobbling lozenges of light, wavy chicken wire shadows on the blue tiles. What is it about swimming pools? Just sit beside one, with a cold beer in your hand and you feel happy. It's like some kind of mesmeric influence. A trance. I said to Yorty once, 'Give everybody their own pool to sit beside and there'd be no more trouble in this world.' The fat moron practically bust a gut.

I myself think it's something to do with the colour of the water. That blue. I always say that they should call that blue 'swimming pool blue'. Try it on your friends. Say 'swimming pool blue' to them. They know what you mean right off. It's a special colour. The colour of tranquility. Got it! TRANQUILITY POOLS . . . Yeah, that's it. Fuck Yorty.

But the only trouble with this particular pool is it's *green*. The man's got green water.

'Hey,' I hear a voice. 'You come for the pool?'

I'm only wearing overalls with AA1 POOLS written across the back in red letters. This guy's real sharp. He comes down the steps from the house, his joint just about covered with a minute black satin triangle. He's swinging a bullworker in one hand. Yeah, he's big. Shoulders like medicine balls, bulging overhang of pectorals. His chest is shiny and completely hairless with tiny brown nipples, almost a yard apart. But his eyes are set close together. I guess he's been using the bullworker on his brain too. I've seen him on the TV. Biff Ruggiero, ex pro-football star.

'Mr Ruggiero?'

'Yeah, that's me. What's wrong wit da pool?'

'You got green water. Your filtration's gone for sure. You got a build up of algae. When was the last time you had things checked out?'

He ignored my question. 'Green water? Shit, I got friends coming to stay tomorrow. Can you fix it?'

'Can you brush your teeth? Sure I can fix it. But you'd better not plan on swimming for a week.'

. . . and this stupid asshole, Biff Ruggiero – you know, pro-footballer? – he hangs around all day asking dumb questions. 'Whatcha need all dat acid for?' So there I am, I'm washing out his friggin cartridges with phosphate tri-soda and all this crap's like coming out. 'Holy Jesus,' says Mr Nobel prize-winner, 'where's all dat shit come from?' 'Jesus,' I laugh quietly to myself, 'he's so dumb he thinks Fucking is a city in China.'

I watch Noelle-Joy get out of bed. She stands for a while rubbing her temples.

'I'm going to take a shower,' she says.

I follow her through to the bathroom.

'It just shows you,' I shout over the noise of the water. 'Those cartridge filters may be cheap but they can be a real pain in the nuts. I told him to put in a sand filter like the one I'm getting. Six-way valve, automatic rinsage –'

Noelle-Joy bursts out of the cabinet, her little stacked body all pink from the shower. She heads back into the bedroom, towels off and starts to dress.

'Hey, baby,' I say. 'Listen. I thought of a great name. Tranquility pools.' I block out the letters in the air. 'Trang. Quil. It. Tee. Tranquility pools. What do you think?'

'Look,' she says, her gaze flinging around the room. 'Ah. I gotta, um, do some shopping. I'll catch up with you later, OK?'

Noelle-Joy moves in. Boy, dames sure own a lot of garbage. She works as a stapler in a luggage factory. We get on fine. But already she's bugging me to get a car. She doesn't like to be seen in the Dodge van. She's a sweet girl, but there are only two things Noelle-Joy thinks about. Money, and more money. She says I should ask Yorty for a raise. I say how am I going to do that seeing I'm already into him for a $5,000 sand filter. She says she wouldn't give the steam off her shit for a sand filter. She's a strong-minded woman but her heart's in the right place. She loves the pool.

'You look after this pool great, you know,' Ruggiero says. I'm de-ringing the sides with an acid wash. We cleaned up the green water weeks ago but we've got a regular maintenance contract with him now.

'I never realized, like, they was so complicated.'

I shoot him my rhyme.

'That's good,' Ruggiero says, scratching his chin. 'Say, you wanna work for me, full time?'

I tell him about my plans. Tranquility pools, the new sand filter, Noelle-Joy.

I come home early. An old lady called up from out on Pacific Palisades. She said her dog had fallen into her pool in the night. She said she was too upset to touch it. I had to fish it out with the long-handled pool sieve. It was one of those tiny hairy dogs. It had sunk to the bottom. I dragged it out and threw it in the garbage can.

'No poolside light, lady,' I said. 'You don't light the way, no wonder your dog fell in. If that'd got sucked into the skimmers you'd have scarfed up your entire filter system. Bust valves, who knows?'

Wow, did she take a giant shit on me. Called Yorty, the works. I had to get the mutt's body out of the trash can, wash it, lay it out on a cushion . . . No wonder I'm red-assed when I get home.

Noelle-Joy's out by the pool working on her tan. Fruit

punch, shades, orange bikini, pushed-up breasts. There's a big puddle of water underneath the sunlounger.

'Hi, honey,' she calls, stretching. 'This is the life, yeah?'

I go mad. 'You been in the water?' I yell.

'What? . . . Yeah. So I had a little swim. So big deal.'

'How many times I got to tell you. The pool's wintering.'

'The pool's been wintering for *three fuckin months*!' she screams.

But I'm not listening. I run into the pool house. Switch on the filters to full power. I grab three pellets of chlorine – no, four – and throw them in. Then I get the sack of soda-ash, tip in a couple of spadefuls, just to be sure.

I stand at the pool edge panting.

'What do you think you're doing?' she accuses.

'Superchlorination,' I say. 'You swam in stagnant water. Who knows what you could of brought in.'

Now she goes mad. She stomps up to me. 'I just *swam* in your fuckin pool, turd-bird! I didn't piss in it or nothing!'

I've got her there. 'I know you didn't,' I yell in triumph. 'Cause I can tell. I got me a secret chemical in that water. *Secret*. Anybody pisses in my pool it turns *black*!'

We made up of course. 'A lovers' tiff' is the expression I believe. I explain why I was so fired up. Noelle-Joy is all quiet and thoughtful for an hour or two. Then she asks me a favour. Can she have a housewarming party for all her friends? There's no way I can refuse. I say yes. We are real close that night.

OTO

OTO. I don't know how we ever got by without OTO, or orthotolodine, to give its full name. We use it in the Aquality Duo Test. That's how we check the correct levels of chlorination and acidity (pH) in a pool. If you don't get it right you'd be safer swimming in a cess pit.

I'm doing an OTO test for Ruggiero. He's standing there crushing a tennis ball in each hand. His pool is looking beautiful. He's got some guests around it – lean, tanned people. Red umbrellas above the tables. Rock music playing from the speakers. Light from the water winking at you. That chlorine smell. That fresh coolness you get around pools.

One thing I will say for Ruggiero, he doesn't treat me like some sidewalk steamer. And the man seems to be interested in what's going on.

I show him the two little test tubes lined up against the colour scales.

'Like I said, Mr Ruggiero, it's perfect. OTO never lets you down. You always know how your pool's feeling.'

'Hell,' Ruggiero says, 'looks like you got to be a chemist to run a pool. Am I right or am I right?' he laughs at his joke.

I smile politely and step back from the pool edge, watch the water dance.

'A thing of beauty, Mr Ruggiero, is a joy forever. Know who said that? An English poet. I don't need to run no OTO test. I been around pools so long I got an instinct about them. I know how they feel. Little too much acid, bit of algae, wrong chlorine levels . . . I see them, Mr Ruggiero, and they tell me.'

'Come on,' Ruggiero says, a big smile on his face. 'Let me buy you a drink.'

Sol Yorty looks like an ageing country and western star. He's bald on top but he's let his grey hair grow over his ears. He lives in dead end East Hollywood. I walk down the path in his back garden with him. Yorty's carrying a bag of charcoal briquettes. His fat gut stretches his lime-green sports shirt skin tight. He and his wife Dolores are the fattest people I know. Between them they weigh as much as a small car. The funny thing about Yorty is that even though he owns a pool company he doesn't own a pool.

He tips the briquettes into his bar-b-q as I explain that I'm going to have to hold back on the sand filter for a month or two. This party of Noelle-Joy is going to make it hard for me to meet the deposit.

'No problem,' Yorty says. 'Glad to see you're making a home at last. She's a . . . She seems like a fine girl.' He lays out four huge steaks on the grill.

'Oh sorry, Sol,' I say. 'I didn't know you had company. I wouldn't have disturbed you.'

'Nah,' he says. 'Just me and Dolores.' He looks up as Dolores waddles down the garden in a pair of flaming orange bermudas and the biggest bikini top I've ever seen.

'Hey sweetie,' he shouts. 'Look who's here.'

Dolores carries a plastic bucket full of rice salad. 'Well hi, stranger. Wanna eat lunch with us? There's plenty more in the fridge.'

I say I've got to get back.

It looks like Noelle-Joy's invited just about the entire workforce from the luggage factory. Mainly guys too, a few blacks and hispanics. The house is crammed with guests. You can't move in the yard. This morning I vacuum-swept the pool, topped up the water level, got the filters going well, and threw in an extra pellet of chlorine. You can't be too sure. Some of Noelle-Joy's friends don't seem too concerned about personal hygiene. Everybody, though, is being real nice to me, Noelle-Joy and I stand at the door greeting the guests. Noelle-Joy makes the introductions. Everyone smiles broadly and we shake hands.

I feel on edge as the first guests dive into the pool. I watch the water slosh over the sides, darkening the No-Skid surrounds. I hear the skimmer valves clacking madly.

Noelle-Joy squeezes my hand. She's been very affectionate these last few days. Now every few minutes she comes on over from talking to her friends and asks me if I'm feeling fine. She keeps smiling and looking at me. But it's what I call her lemon smile – like she's only smiling with her lips. Maybe she's nervous too, I think, wondering what her friends from the luggage factory will make of me.

I have to say I'm not too disappointed though, when I'm called away by the phone. It's from Mr Ruggiero's house. Something's gone wrong, there's some sort of sediment in the water. I think fast. I say it could be a precipitation of calcium salts and I'll be there right away.

I clap my hands for silence at the poolside. Everyone stops talking.

'I'm sorry folks,' I say, 'I have to leave you for a while. I got an emergency on. You all just keep right on having a good time. I'll be back as soon as I can. Bye now.'

Traffic's heavy at this time of the day. We've got a gridlock at Western Avenue and Sunset. I detour round on the Ventura Freeway, out down through Beverly Glen, back on to Sunset and on in to Brentwood.

I run down the back lawn to the pool. I can see Ruggiero and some of his friends splashing around in the water. Stupid fools. The hispanic manservant tries to stop me but I just lower my shoulder and bulldoze through him.

'Hey!' I shout. 'Get the fuck out of that water! Don't you know it's dangerous? Get out, everybody, get out!'

Ruggiero's muscles launch him out of the pool like a dolphin.

'What's goin' on?' He looks angry and puzzled. 'You ain't a million laughs you know, man.'

I'm on my knees peering at the water. The other guests have clambered out and are looking around nervously. They think of plagues and pollution.

In front of my nose the perfect translucent water bobs and shimmies, nets of light wink and flash in my eyes.

'The sediment,' I say. 'The calcium salts . . . didn't somebody phone . . . ?'

By the time I get back I've been away for nearly an hour and a half. She worked fast, I have to admit. Cleaned out everything. She and her friends, they had it all planned. I'd been deep-sixed for sure.

There was a note. YOU MAY NO A LOT A BOUT POOLS BUT YOU DONT NO SHIT A BOUT PEPLE.

I don't want to go out to the yard but I know I have to. I walk through the empty house like I'm walking knee deep in wax. The yard is empty. I can see they threw everything in the pool – the loungers, the tables, the bamboo cocktail bar, bobbing around like the remains from a shipwreck. Then all of them standing in a circle round the side, laughing, having their joke.

I walk slowly up to the edge and look down. I can see my reflection. The water's like black coffee.

Yorba Linda. It's just off the Riverside Expressway. I'm

working as a cleaner at the public swimming pool. Open air, Olympic sized.

Things had to the the after when he heard from Ruggiero. Sol said he had no choice, he was sorry but he would 'have to let me go'.

I sold up and moved out after the party. That pool could never be the same after what they had done in it. I don't know – it had lost its innocence, I guess.

Funny thing happened. I was standing on Sunset and a van halted at an intersection. It was a Ford, I think. It was blue. I didn't get a look at the driver, but on the side, in white letters, was TRANQUILITY POOLS. The van drove off before I could get to it. I'm going to file a complaint. Somebody's stolen my name.

THE SOUTH AFRICAN COUPLE

Giles Gordon

The new couple in the street, at number six, were South African. The Websters, who'd gone to stay with their parents near Oxford – whether it was Hazel's or Brian's mother and father who lived there I do not know, I never remember things like that – had told us before they moved out. They didn't take their furniture with them, not that there was much in the house, there wasn't. They didn't collect possessions (or possess collections) and preferred to eat off the floor and sit on cushions, as it were. Still, the new couple took over what was described as a furnished house.

We wouldn't have known, just by looking, that they were South African, though perhaps we would have done had we heard them speak, had they addressed each other and been overheard. The South African accent is quite distinctive, if you can identify it. They weren't Black or anything like that. Not South African in that sense.

Brian and Hazel, with their children Lucy and Lucifer (I don't know the boy's real name, he was somewhat impish and familiarly called Lucifer by the other children in the *cul-de-sac* of fourteen terraced houses, seven on each side of the road), felt they should be near to granddad, whichever granddad he was, during what were likely to be his last months around. Caspar the Dalmatian – was he white with black spots or black with

21

white areas painted over and around the black? – went with them. He'd always seemed constricted in the city. They'd let their house for six months to the South African couple, so Hazel had told Anne at number one, and Anne had discreetly disseminated the news.

Everyone called them the South African couple. Couple, did I say? There are couples and couples, of course there are, but I'm not sure – which means I don't know – whether the man and the girl, young woman I ought to call her, she looked about twenty-five, were both South African. If only one was I don't know which, presumably the man but maybe not. Man and woman, yes. Husband and wife, no. And more of that in a moment.

It seemed to take them the best part of a week, four or five days anyway, to unpack their belongings from the pile, the mountain of tea chests that grew rather than diminished in the tiny patch of front garden. The tea chests kept coming. Presumably the South African couple weren't gardeners by experience or inclination because in their efforts to assemble a larger and larger heap of tea chests in the space between street and house they buried the flowers, obliterated them rather than placed the tea chests one at a time carefully on the garden, on grass or earth where no plants were in evidence. Our house, number nine, was immediately opposite theirs, one hundred and fifty feet away, and those days whenever I chanced to glance out of the window there they were, the South African couple, stretching deep down into tea chests, extracting objects of varying size and shape, mostly wrapped in brown paper. Everything within the silver foil of the chests seemed to be wrapped, whether china or ornaments or books or whatever it all was. There was no way of telling, at least from where I stood – not that I looked *especially*, you understand, or often, just that I sometimes happened to be looking out – what all those objects were which were being transported up the front stairs, into the guts of the house. It was as well that the Websters' house was modestly furnished.

It was Bill Badger at number four (his real name isn't Bill but Archie but everyone calls him Bill) who told me that the South African couple weren't husband and wife, not in any legal sense. He (the South African, not Bill) had another wife, a wife I mean, who lived – as it happened – just around the corner, in the main street, Borrowdale Crescent. During the week his two children, who looked as if they were about eight and ten, one of each sex, lived with their mother, his wife (heaven knows whether *she* was South African), and on Saturday mornings they would swing round the corner on their bicycles and dismount outside number six, and spend Saturday and Sunday with their father and his new friend, and return on their bicycles to their mother on Sunday night. So he only had them for one night each week, Saturday night. Bad luck if he liked children, his own children especially. Fancy not seeing more of them in their formative years. Maybe it was his girl friend who didn't take much to other people's children.

It's not a weekend I want to tell you about though, or about his children, or about all those objects in the tea chests. It's about a particular Thursday evening. Or Thursday night, depending when you consider evening becomes night, if the distinction is important to you. It was May of this year, the first remotely warm evening following the first warm day we'd experienced since last summer. Our three children had reluctantly and eventually gone to bed but later even than usual as the genial, velvety evening, spring and summer rising at once, had caused them unconsciously to linger, not wanting to miss a moment. Who could assume that tomorrow wouldn't be wet? It usually was.

At five past midnight Maddie said she was going to bed. Maddie's my wife. A schoolday tomorrow, she said, throwing away the evening paper. For the children, she meant. Not a Saturday or a Sunday, so we'd all have to be up early. Work to be done, and not only by schoolchildren. What sort of work the South African couple did I couldn't make out, they always seemed to be unpacking tea chests. Unless this was part of their annual holiday.

Maddie fed the cats, then Henny scuttled and skidded her way through the cat flap by the kitchen door out into the cool night, followed by the older, more lumbering and less neurotic Plato. (Fancy calling a cat Plato, a relative had once said. Not so odd as calling a philosopher Plato, I'd replied.) The drawbridge, guillotine-like, clanged down. I locked the back, then the front door, and Maddie went up to the bathroom. I looked in at the children, and turned off Harry's transistor and observed whether the mice had sufficient water to survive the night. They had. I followed Maddie into the bathroom.

Having washed and brushed what remained of my teeth (I joke, up to a point. I'd just had a tooth crowned, porcelain not gold, and the dentist said it couldn't be done on the National Health which was what really rankled), I walked up to our bedroom. I'd turned the lights off in the hall and on the landing, yet there was enough light filtering in from the street, both from the general orange film of light throughout the city and from our solitary street light, electricity converted from gas. Light reached our bedroom too, I noticed, from the bedroom of number six opposite. One curtain was drawn shut, the other left open. It surprised me because the

Websters had always pulled the curtains across at night before they switched a light on.

I walked towards the window to close our curtains, quite able to see well enough in the dark. I glanced across at the room opposite, assuming someone had left the light on and there was no one there, although I couldn't be certain – not that, either way, it particularly crossed my mind – because from my vantage point about two-thirds of the width of the pink painted front of the house, the same as ours, was taken up by wall and plaster, not by the two windows.

Just then, when my hand was on the curtain and I was about to draw it shut, a woman, the South African woman (if she was South African), appeared in one of the windows. I don't mean that she was looking out, out into the street or across the road or up into the night sky. She seemed oblivious of the outside world, to any existence beyond or apart from her actions of the moment. She was concentrating upon something, perhaps her own face in a mirror if there was a mirror in the room. It was a face worth concentrating upon at that time of night or any other time and if you owned the face a mirror would have to suffice. I could see this, although my eyesight wasn't what it once had been. (I mean, I had to wear spectacles.)

As I watched – you do understand, don't you, I wasn't watching particularly, I'd just happened to be there, about to close the curtains – I could see the woman properly, the shape of her body a bit, not only her silhouette against the blaze of light in the bedroom. She began to undress, took off a garment or two (she hadn't that many on, it was as I've said a warm day) and was standing in her bra and panties. Knickers. Black they were, very tasty pieces of lace or whatever with little holes in them as if placed there by minute pastry cutters. I wasn't that close but that's how they looked. Elegant. Sophisticated.

I said to Maddie, who by this time was in bed behind me, waiting for me to close the curtains and get between the sheets: 'I didn't know that women still wore bras,' to which there was no reply. Women don't appreciate remarks like that. In a way you can't blame them. Later, when I told my friend Dannie about that, he said: 'Now we know what Maddie wears. Or rather doesn't wear,' and laughed. It was a few seconds before I realized what he meant, and what I'd said. Bit of a giveaway.

I don't easily feel embarrassed, and there's little point in blushing in the dark, yet I felt that the South African woman (okay, if she was South African) should have been aware of what she was doing, exposing herself to. Maybe she was used to the plains, what are they called, the veld, and no one for miles. I might have telephoned her if I'd had the number and suggested she drew the curtains but she'd have had to put her clothes on or at least a dressing gown, and I didn't know if she had one, I hadn't seen one, to answer the telephone.

She was taking off – no, had taken off; that was quick – her bra and, do you know, her small and sensible breasts – lovely colour, bare flesh colour (does that surprise you?) – stood there, or whatever breasts do, for all the world and me alone to see. And then, in the next moment it seemed, she bent down and extracted her legs from her knickers, fastidiously kicked her way out. That's one way of looking at it. The other is that she pulled her knickers down her legs. Either way, the result was achieved, the purpose plain. She stood undressed, and ever so good she looked with her contours and the right amount of flesh, with all that electric light around her as if she was providing the light bulb with the wherewithal to burn.

Then she bent down to pick something or other off the floor, something like that. And her breasts turned away and I saw her back and her buttocks and her thighs moved and she was a proper nude, lovely, like a Matisse or a Rembrandt or something great, unique. Completely unexpected. Beautiful. That's it, beautiful.

She remained framed in the window for a few seconds, then chanced (so it seemed) to glance out before moving away, out of my vision. Presumably she'd gone to bed, or somewhere. Was her mouth moving? Was she saying something to someone?

I backed further into the darkness of our bedroom, which was dark only from the outside, looking in, as if I was afraid I'd be revealed, that a light behind *me* might be turned on.

Then, as I say, she was gone. I still looked, a few seconds more – I hadn't yet brought myself to draw the curtains, you understand – when a man, the South African, appeared in the window, peered out and across the soft darkness, into our bedroom, so it seemed, into my eyes. His mouth moved with disdain, more than a twitch, a leer, I could make it out that clearly, and he closed the curtain sharply as if to blot me out. As I've said, my eyesight isn't altogether what it once was but I had the distinct feeling that he'd known I was watching, and hadn't done anything about it.

I closed our curtains, and undressed. The image of her body, of every female nude ever seen, occupied my mind.

'Funny people, South Africans,' I said to Maddie as I got into bed beside her.

Just my luck. She was asleep.

A SOLDIER'S TALE

Carl MacDougall

Maybe it's the way I'm made. That's what Mr Donaldson said. He's the padre, so he ought to know what he's talking about. He said I should pray. He said I should ask God to remove the stain. I tried. But it didn't work. I don't know if I'm doing it right. It seems like talking to yourself. I told Mr Donaldson. I told him I couldn't pray. He said, Keep trying. He said the answer lay within me.

That time, the time between deciding to do it and doing it, is the good time; when I think it's going to be different. It never is. Maybe I do it because I think it's going to be different.

I always think things are going to be different. I thought the Army would be different. I thought the people would be different. I thought the officers would be different. And I thought Ireland would be different. They're not. They're just the same.

Big McDonald said my trouble is that I try to be different. He said I wasn't like one of the boys. When I asked him what the boys were like, he punched me. That's what they're fucken like, he said.

Then at the farm, the first time; I only did it because of him, because he was there, because he made me. Big McDonald could make you do anything. You don't know him.

Three of us, McDonald, me and another guy, went to check it out; a farm, away in the middle of nowhere. We were on patrol. Two Saracens. It started to rain as we turned along a side road that didn't go anywhere at first; then we came to a valley, more of a hollow and there were three farms off the road. We stopped and the main patrol stayed at the road end. The sergeant told the three of us to check it out. He sent groups to the other farms and told us to hurry up. There'll be nothing there, he said.

It was drizzling and I thought how nice and quiet the place looked as we walked up the lane. The buildings lay in a sort of circle, in a huddle and the light shone through the drizzle onto the wet slate roofs. The three of us walked up the lane and into the farmyard. The place looked deserted, quiet.

We looked in the barns and outbuildings, places like that. There was nothing. Then McDonald kicked the back door in. I went in after him and the other guy waited in the yard.

McDonald said, Fenians, when he saw a picture of the Sacred Heart up above the fireplace in the living-room. We used to have one in our house. The old man never bothered. She can put up any kind of picture she likes, he said.

The girl was locked in the upstairs bathroom with a cat. McDonald kicked the door in. O, Mary Jesus and Joseph, she said. Help me. McDonald told me to see if anyone else was in the house. I looked everywhere. I even looked in the attic and under the stairs. The place was empty.

McDonald took the girl into a bedroom and told me to tell the other guy we were giving the place a going over. I shouted down to the yard. He was sitting by the barn, sheltering and having a smoke. He didn't reply when I shouted. He just turned and looked up at me; he nodded, closed his eyes and leaned his head against the wall.

McDonald's gun clicked as he played with the safety catch. The girl was on the edge of the bed holding the cat. She let go and it ran away. He told me to keep cover.

I didn't like to watch. The girl's eyes were open. She was biting her lip and sobbing. It sounded funny, like the noise a train makes rattling on the railway lines.

Your turn, he said. When I looked at him I knew I'd have to do it. Go on, he said. You know what it's for, don't you.

I don't remember much about it. McDonald kept his gun at her head and I closed my eyes. Afterwards I remember thinking, I've done it, so that's what it's like; stuff like that.

Big McDonald told me not to tell anyone. We left her lying on the bed and closed the door. When we got down to the yard McDonald said, Nothing there, to the other guy and the three of us walked back down the road. I don't remember if it was raining or not. Whenever I thought about it I felt funny, as if I wanted it to happen again. Two weeks later a patrol was ambushed on that same road.

I didn't tell about that time or any other time. It happened again, in fact it happened quite a lot and always in the same way. That was why I went to see the padre. I wanted to tell him but couldn't. Instead I told him about the Girl In The Park. Jesus. You should have seen her, the Girl In The Park.

I was home on leave and fed up as usual; fed up being home, fed up that nothing had changed. My mother and father were still fighting. He's a Protestant, she's a Catholic and they argue all the time, mostly about the fact that we were brought up Protestants. They should have had my faith, she says. You weren't bothered at the time, says he. I didn't know then, she says. I was only sixteen. How was I supposed to know that, how was I supposed to know how important your faith is. I know now, she says. I know now. Too late, says he. I know that, she says. I know that now. Look at him. And she points at me. He's a soldier, my father says. He has to go where they send him. It isn't right, she says. He should never have joined up. He had to, he says, my father, looking at her, never at me. He had to. There's no other work for him. I get fed up after a while. I think it's going to be different, but it's always the same.

At first I just went out, walked around and went home when I was hungry. I started going to the pub, sometimes to the betting shop, but these guys are always skint. They tap you and never pay you back; or else they cadge booze and fags off you. I stopped going.

One morning I wakened just after six and didn't go back to sleep because I thought I was in the barracks instead of being home on leave. I was up; I had my socks and trousers on before I realized where I was. Then I thought, what difference does it make, so I stayed up. I had some tea and went out for a walk. Don't ask me why, I don't know why, no reason; I wandered into the park.

It was weird. Creepy. No one was around. The trees looked taller than usual. It's a strange feeling, being in a place that's usually full of people when there's no one around. You wonder if you're in the right place. The paths look as if they're never going to end because they don't go anywhere and if it's a clear day the landscape and sky look like a photograph. Of course it's different if it's raining. There are some days you'd be better not seeing the way they begin. I've been to the park at first light in all weathers, but this time, this first time, I was wandering around as if I was a character in a film or in a dream, except I don't dream too well. Maybe a dream sequence in a film.

A white cloudy mist lay in patches and everything looked as if it was separated, cut into two or even three parts by the mist. The park is divided anyway. At the entrance there's nothing but concrete; the paths and the flower-beds, even the benches are concrete. Then there's a wide semi-circle of flowers built into a mound with concrete edging and beyond that is the park itself; just a big field really, surrounded by trees and hedges, dotted with flower-beds and clumps of bushes.

I sat on a bench near the entrance and rolled a fag. The sun was up and all that mist and stuff made the park look very spooky, like a sleeping animal, as if something beneath the ground was ready to jump out, to grab you and take control.

She came running out of the mist. I was looking down at the park when I saw her. At first I didn't think it was anyone, just a flash of colour by the trees. If I wasn't a soldier I wouldn't have bothered, but I've been trained to recognize that sort of thing, to look for sudden movements, to see the unexpected in a familiar surrounding.

She ran by the edge of the field and was lost in a clump of mist. I stood on the bench to see her. She ran out of the mist and along by the trees. When I saw her I felt something funny, as if I'd drunk hot tea and it hadn't reached my stomach, but had stayed in my chest and spread itself out across my body. It was a nice feeling.

Jesus Johnny. That's what Big McDonald said when I told him. I didn't really tell him. I only said I'd seen this girl I fancied and he said, What's she like? I said I didn't know. I hope she's not a Tim, he said. I told him I hadn't spoken to her and he said, Jesus Johnny. Why don't you speak to her? I told him she was running and he laughed. No use for you, he said. He was right. I couldn't run a mile to save myself. I could do with losing two, probably three stones. Beer.

She wore her hair up and even though it was tied with a ribbon there were these little bits of blonde hair hanging down beside her ears. She wore a T-shirt, shorts and gym shoes. That's all. I'm sure that's all. I watched her and I'd swear she'd nothing on underneath.

It was good watching her. Hardly anyone looks good running, they don't look as if they're built for it, especially women. The only people I've seen who look good are the skinny blokes who do cross country. One of the units challenges everybody to a sports day and the big event is the cross country; people bet on it, though they'd get jankers if they were caught. You always know it's going to happen because these guys are out training weeks in advance. You see them running, usually in pairs. They always look as if they're going to die, skinny men with sweaty vests and bony chests, their mouths open, eyes staring straight ahead. Their whole body quivers every time their feet hit the ground. They don't look as if they could do anything else; mile after mile, running. Then you come home on leave and see some fat guy in a nicely pressed track suit peching and blowing; or some fat woman, a housewife probably, with blanco on her shoes. Makes me sick. But Her. You should have seen Her.

When we were at school we went to the ballet. An English teacher took us. It was free. Just as well, otherwise nobody would have gone. It was a good laugh at first. Somebody said the men were bent because they wore make up and anyway they looked bent. I was bored most of the time. I couldn't understand what it was for or what they were supposed to be doing. But I don't think these guys were bent. For one thing, you should have seen them jump. Then they lifted the girls above their heads and ran around with them like that. You can't be all that queer if you can pick up someone

33

who weighs seven or eight stone, maybe more, and carry them all over the place, running and making it look easy.

I liked it when the girls ran; just watching the way their backsides moved when they ran off stage, the funny way they ran on tip-toe with their hands and arms behind them and their faces up towards the sky as if they couldn't see where they were going. That's the way she ran, the Girl In The Park. And she looked good.

I went to the park every morning and she was always there, even when it was raining. I worked out what time she came, twenty-five past seven, and even tried to work out where she was going. I thought of following her, but I couldn't run a mile if you paid me. Hopeless.

Three nights before I was due to go back I got drunk. I didn't mean to get drunk, it just happened. There were a lot of different things going on. My mother and father had a fight and it was just like it used to be. I thought they were too old for that, but I was wrong. He came in drunk and she started shouting. He punched her and threw a holy picture out the window and that made her mad.

The fight made me think about going back. I'm usually pleased, but this time I thought about the Girl In The Park and I didn't want to go back. Then I realized I'd never spoken to her. I made up my mind to try to stop her, to say Hello.

I went to the pub because the atmosphere in the house was terrible; there was just an awful silence. Sometimes I drink a lot and it never bothers me, other times I get drunk on two pints. I ordered a pint of export and when I'd finished it I felt myself beginning to go, you know that funny way when you can feel your nerves. I don't remember getting home, in fact I can only remember bits of what happened.

After the pub we went to someone's house. I was sick

and went for a walk. When I got back a woman opened the door for me and we sat in the kitchen talking and drinking beer. I told her about my life, about Big Mc-Donald and the Girl In The Park. I don't think I told her anything else. I hope not. I couldn't have because she gave me a cuddle. I didn't know what to do. I was embarrassed. It didn't last long. In one way I wish it had lasted longer, but in another I'm glad it didn't. People in the sitting room were listening to Dylan. I quite like Dylan. I like the way he laughs at the end of 'All I Really Want To Do'. It's a good laugh, as though he means it; but I don't like the song where he says Join The Army If You Fail. It's all right for him to say that, he doesn't know what it's like. Nothing happened, though I don't remember getting home.

But I must have got home, for that's where I wakened just after six. If I was lucky I'd had four hours' sleep. I dreamed I was wakened and the bed felt like a Saracen. Then before I wakened I dreamed about her, so I made my mind up. I would talk to her that morning. Definitely.

I walked to the park and stood by the trees. It was a bright morning. The sky was pink and the trees looked black. The birds were making a racket, crows and sea-gulls mostly. I stood near to where I thought she'd come from. It seemed like ages. Then I heard a twig snap and I heard her coming; I could hear her breathing and hear her run. She came out of the trees about six yards from where I was standing. I shouted, Hello. She turned and saw me. Then she smiled, she smiled and waved her hand in a strange way, as if she was drying her nail varnish. She raised her arm above her head and fluttered her hand. And kept on running. She didn't stop and she didn't say anything. She waved her hand.

Next morning on my way to the park I decided to stop her. I'd stop her and say, Hello. Then I'd tell her how I came to see her and I'd ask her name. I'd tell her I was a soldier home on leave and ask if she'd like to go to the pictures or go for a drink or something. She'd say, Yes. And I'd say, Great. Then we'd meet and go for a drink and go to the pictures and we wouldn't touch or hold hands or anything like that, we'd just walk together and talk about the picture we'd seen. And I'd walk her home to where she lived in a big house in the clean part of the city. At the gate at the foot of the drive I'd thank her for coming out with me and tell her I was going back to my regiment in Northern Ireland and ask if she'd write to me. She'd smile and say, Of course. Then I'd turn to go away, back down the street, but I'd stop at the corner, just by the lamp post; I'd turn and see her still standing there. I'd look and smile and feel like I've never felt before when she waved to me.

It would be awful waiting for her letters. Then the first would arrive. On pink paper. Smelling of scent. I'd read her nice handwriting and write a letter back to her, taking care to write properly, to spell the words right. I'd tell her I missed her and I'd say how much I was looking forward to seeing her again when I came home. She'd tell me to take care of myself and ask how long I had to do.

Then I'd get a weekend pass. It would mean we could only have Saturday night together, but I could tell her all about me and my mother and father and the rest of the family and how I couldn't take her to meet them because of where they lived and what they were like. And she'd say, It's you I'm interested in, not your family.

When I got back I'd tell Big McDonald to get stuffed. I'd even fight him if he pushed me. But he wouldn't do that because of the hold I have over him and he knows it. I'd tell him we were quits and I wasn't going to do that sort of thing any more because I'd found a nice girl who loved me.

I was shivering when I got to the park. There's a big supermarket on the corner across the street, opposite the entrance. As I passed I saw myself in the shop window. I had to stop to see that it was me. It didn't look like me. I didn't look the way I thought I looked, or how I felt. I looked rough. Dirty. I needed a wash and a shave and my hair was greasy. I didn't look smart either. I'd an old pair of trainer shoes and wide-bottomed trousers that were out of fashion and hadn't been pressed. My T-shirt said I AM A VIRGIN in big letters and Islander in small letters. My checked sports jacket looked crumpled. Nothing matched anything else. I don't usually bother about that sort of thing, but I bothered about it when I saw myself looking a mess in the supermarket window. It bothered me because I thought it would bother her.

I wanted to go home and change. But I didn't have any nice clothes to change into. And if I went home I'd miss seeing her. When I left the window I knew I couldn't talk to her and was nervous about what I'd say anyway.

So I went to the park to see her for the last time. I stood up by the flower-beds where I always stood. At about twenty past seven I walked down towards the park. I'll never forget it. Everything looked crisp and new and clean in the sunshine, as if I shouldn't be there.

When she came out from the trees I wanted to cry. I felt stupid and I felt clumsy. She looked like a star. She was wearing a blue Adidas sweat shirt and blue shorts. She had a pink ribbon in her hair. Her face was flushed. She stopped when she saw me. She smiled and put her hands on her hips, smiling all the time as if I was supposed to say something. Her teeth were white and even. Her eyes were blue. Jesus.

Christ Almighty. She stood there breathing heavily and looking at me. I tried. I tried to speak, tried to say something, but the words wouldn't come. She looked so lovely, like a nice dream standing there. She didn't stay long, long enough to gather her breath. There were beads of sweat on her forehead, strands of her hair were wet and the sides of her mouth fell as she shrugged her shoulders, turned and ran down the edge of the trees and across the grass on that clear, clear morning, disappearing through the bushes on the other side of the park. Before she disappeared she raised her arm above her head and jiggled her fingers. She must have known I hadn't moved. I stood where I was, expecting to see her again. But I never saw her again.

I went back a day early. Big McDonald was angry and said he wanted to get someone then and there. I didn't tell him I was angry because we weren't angry about the same things. Tims, he said. That's all they're good for. They like it. They breed like rabbits. He kept on about it. I tried to talk, tried to tell him about the Girl In The Park. Jesus Johnny.

About a week later we were out on patrol and the Saracen ran over a dog in a farmyard. We looked at it lying there with a squint leg. McDonald didn't say anything, he just walked up and shot the dog. A woman started shouting at him because he'd killed her pet. When he walked away the woman complained to the officer. The officer spoke to McDonald, who looked at the officer and said, The dog was howling and I can't stand tears.

That night he told me what was going to happen. I didn't believe him. But it happened.

Whatever I tell you to do, do it, he said. Or else I'll kill you. He used to spit in my food. Once he spat in my face, for nothing. He used to punch and kick me on the body and take money from me.

Five times he did it and made me keep guard. I didn't mean to. He made me. He made me do it. In the back of a van to a woman we were supposed to be interrogating.

He was promoted and that made matters worse. He did everything he did before and he made me do his duties as well as my own. I thought about it for a long time before I went to see the Major. I told him I wasn't shopping McDonald. I told him I wanted a transfer and only told him when he forced me by asking why I wanted the transfer. All the time he asked me, Why? I told him about McDonald. Except for one thing. I never told him about that. I only told what he did to me.

I suppose it's fairly common, said the Major. I don't really know. What I do know is that Lance Corporal McDonald is an excellent soldier with a first-class record, which is more than we can say for you.

He turned me down. McDonald found out I'd applied and came up to me one night when I was sleeping. I felt his hand on my face and opened my eyes. He was looking at me. He said he was going to kill me. You won't know when, he said. I could tell he meant it. I could tell by the way he looked at me. I couldn't sleep and went to church to get a kip. That gave me the idea of talking to Mr Donaldson, the padre.

I nearly told him. I said I'd done something I didn't want to do. I said I was forced into doing it. He said I should pray to have the stain removed. He told me to remember I was a soldier and not to let the flag down.

Next time I was home I spent the whole leave arguing with the old man. He'd got a dog and I hated it. I used to look at it and wish it was dead. I used to batter it with a stick so that it trembled when it saw me and ran under the table. One night when I was drunk I punched some old geezer in a pub because he was annoying me, singing when I'd told him to shut up.

That happened in the pub where I met her. She was drunk and had red hair, black at the roots. She had lipstick on her tooth and her nails were bitten. Her tights were ripped and there were cigarette burns on her skirt. I bought her a drink, then got a carry out. We went to her place, up a smelly close. There's bits I can't remember. Booze.

What's the matter? she said. Can you no do it, son?

It's as if there was a flash, as if a light had been turned on or something. I imagined Big McDonald was making me do it. I suppose it's the way I'm made. I know it isn't right and I don't like it any more than I know what happens. This time with that woman was the first time I'd done it on my own, when I wasn't forced. Looking back, I know it wouldn't have happened if I hadn't been drunk.

She was laughing and I hit her. As soon as I hit her I felt like doing it. And the more I hit her the more I felt like doing it. I did it while she was crying. When I got home there was blood on my clothes from where I'd hit her. I told my mother I'd been in a fight. I suppose the woman was all right. She was crying to herself when I left, saying, Mammydaddy, Omygod.

The blood made me think of the Girl In The Park. I don't know why. It just did. I don't know how I feel about her now. I went back, but never saw her. Just as well I suppose. I hardly think of her now. Only once in a while. It usually happens if I see someone like her, but that doesn't happen very often because there isn't anyone like her. I bet she's married now. I bet she has kids and never even runs.

Doing it on my own made a difference. It had happened and that was that. I learned a lot. I learned not to drink for one thing. I don't drink; well, hardly ever. It's dangerous if I drink; it's as if I lose control.

The last time I got drunk was just after I got back, after that time with the woman. I got drunk and didn't go to my billet. I'd lifted a brick, so I went to see McDonald, to tell him, to warn him, to get him to leave me alone. He was sleeping. His mouth was lying open and he was snoring like a pig. I hit him with the brick and hit him and hit him. I kept hitting him. He struggled but I'd got in first. The funny thing is that he never shouted, never screamed. There was just a long muffled grunt and some moaning and groaning. I didn't do much damage, not as much as I thought I'd done. I only fractured his skull. I went to see him in hospital and gave him the brick as a present.

About two weeks after he came out of hospital he was blown up. We never found out for sure, but the UDA are supposed to have done it. One guy lost a leg and another just got injuries. The papers said Big McDonald was a hero. So did the telly. We laughed when we saw that. Someone cut it out and stuck it up on the noticeboard. The Major picked me to be in the Guard of Honour at his funeral. That was a laugh.

I don't do what he did. Never. I only do it when I'm on leave. Even then I'm careful. I hire a car.

I don't always do it when I decide to do it. Sometimes I have to think about it. Sometimes it takes a week, maybe even a fortnight. I don't always notice how long it takes. It depends on how I'm feeling. Sometimes I look and decide then and there.

I could be driving, see someone, think about it, then forget. Or decide not to. It's a risk. I know it's a risk and I've got to feel as though I can do it.

You've got to be careful. Women are very suspicious. They don't speak to strangers, especially strangers in cars. But they don't need to know you very long before they'll go into a car with you. It happens all the time.

You see it in pubs; people standing talking, they've just met and half an hour later he's running her home. It could be anybody. So I've got to break the ice.

If I see someone, I'll draw up to the kerb, stop the car, get out and shout, Mary. She always turns, unsure if it's her. And when she turns I'll try a little smile, but mostly I'll look apologetic. I say, Sorry. Gosh, I am sorry. I thought you were someone else. I only saw you from the back and thought; well anyway. I'm sorry.

Then I smile and get going. Never hang about. All the time I'm watching to see how she's taking it. You can tell from her eyes. Sometimes she says something or she smiles as I get in the car. If she does that, it's certain.

I draw away, not too far and I always stop within sight of her. If I've judged it right, and I've never been wrong yet, if I've judged it right, we're on. I look awkward, stand by the passenger door, smile as she approaches and say, Look. I'm sorry to bother you again, but it seems silly. If you were Mary I'd offer you a lift. Which way are you going?

She must be going a long way, across town, something like that. If she's only going a short distance, round the corner or whatever, it's no good. It's about fifty-fifty. She might say, No thanks. She might say, It's okay. She might say, I'm not going far. And someone actually said, I'm going in here, and disappeared into a shop. But half the time she'll say, That's really nice. Thanks very much. In she gets and away we go.

You learn to assess it properly. It depends on how I'm feeling, but I usually like to talk about where they stay, boy friends, work and so on. I always have the radio going. I tell them a little about myself, or drop hints so they'll ask. Sometimes I tell them I'm a pilot. Sometimes I'm a journalist. Or a commercial artist, something like that. And just when the conversation's going well and it would be a shame to break it up, I'll apologize for the fact that I'm driving slowly.

I like them to feel sorry for me. It's easier in the long run. So I'll tell them how my girl friend was killed in a car crash ten days before we were to be married, how I was driving and how I can never forgive myself. I know I'm not to blame, I say. But you can't help thinking. What a shame, they say when I tell them the whole sad story about the little row; nothing much, every couple has rows. I know I'm not to blame. I'm over it now, I tell them. But it took a while. Two years. It's a long time. Sometimes I tell them I met her when we were jogging in the park. Then I say, Look at me. I haven't run since. And smile about it.

One or two have asked if I've met anyone else. When I say, No, they say, Don't worry. You will, or, I hope you will; I hope you do, something like that.

When they feel sorry for me they also like me, so I say, I don't know why I told you that. I hardly ever mention it. You remind me of her, just the way you turn your head. I feel I can talk to you.

That's nice, they say, and I change the subject to some film or other, a good TV programme, something, lots of jokes and funny stuff. I never swear, never talk about sex or anything like that. If they do I get rid of them quickly. I talk about happy subjects, usually their holidays. Where they've been or where they're going.

The thing is to keep talking so they're at their ease. If they're at their ease, they'll think you're a nice person. I suppose they're usually nice people from nice areas, or they're people who want to live in nice areas. Good people. Sometimes I think she's a nice person and I just drive her home and make a date or something. Of course I never turn up and she's left wondering what happened to the nice, kind interesting person who went out of his way to give her a lift home, instead of the other way.

You've got to be careful. They're expecting you to take them straight home, so you've got to watch the traffic lights and try not to stop. They might suddenly panic and jump out, so you've got to keep moving all the time. That's why you've got to get them to like you, so's they won't jump out. So you've got to watch the lights, avoid reds and jump the ambers. Above all, you must keep moving.

And you must pick your time. You must learn to wait for the right moment; getting dark with the streets empty of people.

And you also have to remember she's getting suspicious. You're no longer in the clean section. No matter where she lives, you always have to pass through a dirty section. It depresses them. They know it's there, but they don't want to be reminded. And you're a stranger, so there's only a certain amount you can talk about before she gets suspicious.

Women are naturally suspicious anyway. And they become more suspicious when a nice, good person drives them through a dirty part of town. Clean people want to stay in the clean section. Dirty people want to stay in the clean section too and that's the reason there's trouble in the world today.

Dirty people ought to stay where they are. They get angry, usually at the wrong people and that's when the trouble starts, killing and the like. No one would mind if they stayed in their own bit and did it to each other. But when they start invading other peoples' property and privacy the clean people get angry. They don't want to know. It's all right to read about it. If the dirty people stayed in their own bit and killed each other and everyone else read about it, no one would bother. They'd say that's all they were good for, no wonder, what else do you expect, and stuff like that. But when they start killing clean people, it's a different story then all right. Clean people feel threatened. They get angry. They want to protect their property. They want to protect themselves and their families; especially the people who were brought up in dirty areas, but who now live in the clean bit. They're worst of all. Clean people want things to stay as they are and dirty people want change. Clean people don't want change because they don't see any need for it. They're frightened of change. They think they're important; they think being clean makes them special, so they like to think they start the changes. They can't imagine change coming from dirty people. They hate that. They hate to think that anything could come from anybody other than themselves. Nothing comes from them. They think they own everything. But they don't. Neither does the Government.

I hate rain. If it's raining I might decide to call the whole thing off. Especially if it looks as if she'll make a run for it. It's hard to tell, but just in case you make sure she's got nowhere to run to.

This is where it changes. This is where she gets worried about where we're going. She doesn't know where we are. There are dirty streets and ruined buildings. Huddles of women bunched on the corners, round-shouldered men smoking. And their children with hopeless faces. The place makes her feel strange so she gets scared. Especially if it's raining. You can tell. It's in her voice and it's in her eyes. She knows what's happening. She knows what's going on. The fear she's always lived with is going to happen to her.

She'll start talking. They all do. Please, she'll say. I've never done it before. Sometimes they become indignant and say, What are you doing? when they know damn well what you're going to do. They always talk.

Always. As if they feel a need to convince me. To try to make me change my mind.

Why do you do this? they say. You're an attractive man. You don't need to do this.

There's a couple of places I use. She usually goes in the back of her own accord. Mostly they're as scared as me. It only takes about ten minutes.

Sometimes they sob. Sometimes they breathe normally. Sometimes they hold their breath. Sometimes they scream and kick. I remember an American thing on TV. We all watched it. Everybody in the barracks watched it. It was a laugh. Just a lot of women feeling sorry for themselves. One woman said it hurt and everybody cheered. It doesn't hurt. It only hurts if they struggle. If they let it happen it doesn't hurt. At the end of this programme they spoke to a couple of guys who were doing time. One said, It's exciting when they scream. Maybe he didn't say that. Maybe I only thought he said it.

Driving back they're quiet. There's always an embarrassed silence, sometimes crying. I take them near to where they're going and tell them the truth. I say, I'm sorry. I didn't mean it to be this way. I like you and I'd like to see you again and for things to work out properly. But they don't. It might be all right for a while. But it would never work out properly.

I say that because I believe it. That's what I believe.

THE SOUND OF
A GAMALAN ORCHESTRA

Ron Butlin

For the third time that day Matthew considered the mobile of delicately worked glass and copper-wire. Then, leaning close, he breathed upon it, creating the slightest whispering noise and a fragmented spectrum. Gradually the condensation evaporated, leaving colourless glass and copper. More than forty years ago he had called the sculpture 'Here I am' – not the kind of title he would use nowadays.

He had been returning from a party about five o'clock one summer's morning, his mind filled with the girl he had just left. The deserted streets, the parked cars, the iron railings, the dawn chorus – all were taking place elsewhere. She alone was happening; and forty years later he could remember only that touching her crinkled red hair was like drawing his hand through fire.

He was so filled with her he wanted to run, to exhaust himself. He wanted to tell someone, to announce her to the whole world. A telephone box stood at the next corner. Perhaps he could call his friend Colin just to say, 'It's me, Matthew, and I'm so very happy here in the big, empty streets at five in the morning.' But no: Colin either wouldn't answer, or would hang up, or, at best, demand explanations – and there was nothing more he wanted to say. Instead, without anger, he kicked in each of the bottom panes of glass. And afterwards he began walking home at a normal pace.

But only for a few yards. He stopped, then returned to look at what he had done. A few moments later he was gathering up the fragments of glass, cautiously prising out the jagged edge-pieces that remained in the frames. Though he was very careful he cut his fingers several times and, to reduce the bleeding, had to carry the glass in his upturned hands which he held just above shoulder-height. This was very tiring and every so often he was forced to rest his elbows against a wall or a pillar-box.

It took nearly an hour to reach home, by which time his arms ached unbearably. He did not go to bed however. Instead, having taken all the glass in one hand, with the other he pulled at the top blanket and spread it on the floor as best he could. Then, thankfully, he laid the broken glass upon it.

Having put the kettle on to boil, Matthew rolled up his sleeves and washed the blood from his hands and arms. When the water was ready he poured it into a basin and began painstakingly to clean each piece of glass.

Apart from two very quick breaks for something to eat he worked continuously through the day until, by the early hours of the following morning, he had finished. Three of his flatmates were still awake and Matthew could still remember their delight at breathing upon his sculpture. Afterwards he had slept for twelve hours.

Matthew replaced 'Here I am' carefully in its position beside some other pieces on a polished wooden shelf and returned to his workbench. This stood in the centre of his studio, the upper storey of a house he himself had designed. It was very quiet here: a good place to spend a working winter, he had thought when first visiting the Alpine village by chance some twenty years ago.

And he always had plenty of work. At other times of the year his base was a large flat in London near the

British Museum. From there he would travel all over the world lecturing, exhibiting and being celebrated. At the moment, however, he was engaged on a small carving – a private commission he had felt certain he would enjoy working on.

His tools were laid out neatly on the table – the various chisels, knives, files and sandpapers he would require. He had spent some considerable time meditating upon the piece and choosing the appropriate wood. From the very start he knew exactly what he wished to do.

Why then was it taking so long? For nearly five weeks he had been fiddling about with this lump of wood, staring at it for hours at a time. He would sit out on the verandah looking at the clouds or at the wind disturbing snow-patterns on the roofs, yet he was always aware of the wood his hands held in his lap. Exploring it, feeling it, caressing it almost, his fingers never stopped trying to coax some life out of, or into, its deadness. And it was not just this piece, he knew; for the last few years he had been struggling without release. Not work, but careful labour.

His sculptures were admired not only by the public, but by many of his fellow-artists: a rare distinction. Women, and sometimes men, beautiful, crazy, understanding gave themselves to him as if they might then sense something they felt denied. To the curious he would answer: 'imagination, persistence and persistence'. They would smile and shake their heads.

Matthew picked up the piece of wood and began sandpapering a ragged edge he had cut in a moment's irritation two days ago. He felt more peaceful now, smoothing, polishing. Every few minutes he stopped and carefully blew away the accumulated dust. Then he resumed his patient work.

What time is it? he wondered. If it was three o'clock

then he could go downstairs and ask Anna if she would like to come for a walk with him. Having been in his studio since eight-thirty that morning he had put in a good six hours, allowing for lunch, which sanctioned a clear conscience for the rest of the day. As there were some people coming to dinner he and Anna would discuss possible menus during the walk, before going down to the village to buy what extras might be required. It was leaving things rather to the last minute, but dinner-parties were often better like that, less formal.

It was just two-thirty. Another half-hour still to go. Matthew sandpapered for a few minutes more then, walking out on to the open balcony, held the wood up above eye-level to catch the full light. He kept his arms raised as long as he could, turning his hands to see every side, but nothing happened. He returned indoors and, having replaced the lump of wood on the bench, sat down in his armchair.

Perhaps he shouldn't have come here at all. He was a sociable man and enjoyed the stimulation of fellow artists dropping in from time to time to talk shop; whereas, up here in the mountains, all he ever heard was the soft rattling of cow-bells from across the valley. He could hardly blame the cow-bells or Mont Blanc – yet he worked as hard as he ever had, perhaps even harder, and nothing happened.

He sat listening to the cow-bells and pretended instead he was listening to a gamalan orchestra. He had heard one while visiting Bali a few years ago, and the sound was really quite similar. His host had given him the captivating description of the orchestra – in fact, but one instrument – as being rather like an immense piano played on by twenty players at once. As he listened it seemed that suddenly he was hearing the cow-bells' sound as shaped in a continuously varying counterpoint to the almost mystic relationship between the players, and between each player and the gamalan.

Excitedly Matthew picked up the pencil and pad of paper from the small table beside him and began sketching the sound of this gamalan orchestra. He encouraged himself by muttering under his breath 'Yes, that's it . . . No, not quite . . . Again.' He tried sketch after sketch 'better, better'. Each seemed to fail differently though he felt he was getting closer. 'No, no . . . Almost' he said and tried again.

After nearly twenty attempts he sat quite still; then, without rising from his chair, gathered up the various sheets that lay within reach. He glanced through them one by one, slowly; but there was nothing – just meaningless lines, curves and smudges. He remained where he was for several minutes staring at the pages on his lap.

It would be after three now. He got up intending to have one more look at the piece he was trying to work on before going downstairs. Instead, for the fourth time that day, he found himself examining 'Here I am'. Affectionately he picked it up, then leant close to breathe upon it and hear its whispered reply. He carried it over to the verandah to enjoy more fully the clear mountain light breaking and re-forming inside it.

The condensation was evaporating gradually, and the colours fading. He raised it higher, his arms began to tremble, yet always there seemed the possibility of another shred of colour if he tilted the piece differently. His whole body began shaking with the strain of holding it up to the light. He became exhilarated. He became certain that something was about to happen. Something miraculous. Suddenly the effort was too great: the sculpture fell to the floor and shattered.

Matthew staggered against the workbench. He rested there for a few minutes to recover his breath. There was broken glass everywhere and he could see at a glance the work was beyond repair. Absently he began picking up some of the pieces. It was then that he realized he was crying.

That was how she found him, Anna was telling their friends that evening when her husband was out of the room making coffee: on his knees amid the fragments of his first sculpture, and in tears.

Matthew, meanwhile, had set the water to boil and stepped out onto the verandah. It pleased him to remain there for a few minutes, listening to the soft rattle of the cow-bells coming from across the valley through the clear night air. It pleased him for the first time in years.

THE BODACHAN

Eona Macnicol

The two children played at soldiers with the plantain tails that grew among the grass. They were waiting until the doctor should come out from the Big House. Lachlan sometimes had to let Mor win, otherwise she would have become discouraged from playing further with him: he chose tender plantains for himself so that hers could cut off their heads – ffp! just the way the real soldiers did in the clan fighting beyond the town. And all the time he munched sorrel leaves to still his stomach's yearning.

But all the time he was on the alert, and as soon as the great door creaked open he was on his feet and running through the courtyard first of all the children to help the groom bring the doctor's horse round. Whoever was lucky enough to hold its head while the groom gave the learned man a heave-up into the saddle might earn a bodle.

He had to be quick to have success. They were all eager for the job; winter is long, and it is a lean time till kail and corn come again. But Lachlan was desperate for it. For where other boys could get work, herding cows, gathering sheep, delving or cutting sticks, he was looked on askance and sent post-haste away. Time was when his pittance was but an addition to his grand-mother's earnings; now, when it had become the main-stay of the household, he could rarely come by anything at all.

Two men came out, Castlehill was with the doctor,

prepared to ride with him as usual for the medicines he should prescribe. The faces of both were grave, the doctor's indeed resentful as if he felt unjustly used because his cures had had so little effect. Lachlan held the horse's head till, grumbling, he was up; then turned to do the same for Castlehill. But the laird with an impatient exclamation thrust him aside and cut at him angrily with his whip so that Lachlan all but tumbled under the horse's hoofs.

He scrambled up little the worse: a fall is no great matter when one is ten years old, skin and pride alike are swift to heal. The groom, Murroch Og, a kindly fellow, before turning away offered consolation. 'You will have to forgive him, *laoghain*! He is in trouble today. They are all in trouble, my Lady Castlehill and the young ladies and all the household.'

'Is the Master so bad then?'

'Bad aye, and worse growing. And the worst of all is, no man of science can find what it is that ails him. If they knew they might hit upon the cure.' He went off muttering, 'A toadskin powdered! A hen's droppings in water! Abh-abh, I would rather suffer illness than treatment of it.'

The children were not greatly interested. They already knew that the young Castlehill, the Master, had returned from the Low Countries gravely ill and with a mysterious illness that would yield to no doctor's skill. His mother's anxious face might sometimes be seen at a window as she waited for yet another medical man to appear. At church too in the laird's loft, supposing one dared to raise one's eyes to it, one could see her and the Master's sisters with their plaids drawn close to hide their faces – although it is against the rule for common folk to hide their faces in church.

That was big folks' trouble. They had their own,

54

which was chiefly lack of food. He and Mor were orphan children, they would have had to travel for their bread had not their grandmother taken them to her. A careful laundress, and not unskilled in the delivering of a child, she had for years earned and had enough to eat. Even when she added fortune-telling to her other skills she was approved and rewarded. But during this last year folk had altered in their regard. Grandmother now had to leave the clean linen outside doors, should she indeed be given the task of laundering it at all, and folk cried out if she came near a childbed. The ill-will towards her extended to himself and Mor, no longer could they count on getting work to do.

This melancholy change had come about since the return of Catrine, their young aunt, her daughter, whom the old woman guarded as if she were her jailer. Poor Catrine, who sat by the fire if there were one or without if there were none, in the darkness of the little house, without speaking, without moving for hours on end, without glow of life, half-dead. How different she was from the rosy dimpling girl who was sewing-maid to my Lady Castlehill, who had come tripping home on light feet on high days and holidays, bringing dainties she had saved from her portion for them. Chicken – goose – sweetmeats. Not to be thought of now.

A bodle would have bought a pat of crowdie to put on their oat bannock, or two or three garvies (sprats) from the Firth.

Fish, that was the thing. If he could not buy them he must catch them. He pulled little Mor up from her picking of daisies and took her, chain and all, to the burn. Here while she played herself he would lie on his rumbling stomach and guddle below the bank for small burn trout.

55

It is hard to remain still while brother is fishing. The burn was like an exciting companion calling her to play. It sang and gurgled and whispered, telling her to look! watch! It was full of treasures. Where it made itself a wide pool there were tiny white flowers swaying on their hidden stems, and water spiders running races with one another.

It was by the pool that she saw it suddenly, the little thing that had a shape like a man's. She could not at first believe her eyes. Such a thing to see inside the burn! It was wedged between two large stones, the boulders that dammed the pool, held fast in the current. If she waded to it – she gave one quick glance towards Lachlan, lost in his fishing, then dipped her feet in. The water was cold – it was still only April – but she scarcely felt its sting. She pulled her ragged gown over her knees and stepped cautiously on to the bed of the stream. The stones were round and smooth, shifting under her feet, but she reached the spot. Her hand felt down the slimy boulders until she touched the little man-like thing. Her fingers closed round it, and she pulled and drew it up out of the water, the little darling, that had a head and a waisted body and arms and legs of clay. Holding it dripping in her hand she climbed up on to the bank with it.

It was naked like a baby. She so greatly missed the baby they had had in the house last summer. Its hands had been like little claws, little pink claws, its face scarcely bigger than an egg but so pretty and complete, with a mouth and tiny nose and close-shut eyes that had thin lines above them where eyebrows would be. If only Catrine had stayed longer in the house the babe would have lived and grown. But one day men came. She Mor had seen them from inside the house, standing before the door tall and terrible, dark in the sunshine. Two elders of the church they were and with them officers of the town. They had called for Catrine Tulloch to come out, and they spent a long time questioning her about the father of the child, and were so angry with her for not answering them that they spoke of banishment. That very night Catrine forestalled them, took the baby and went away.

Now Catrine was back. She had almost died of the winter's cold. And the baby had died.

She was back in their house. But no one must know of it. For if they knew and the news got out, the officers would come again, and they would be angrier than ever, not only because the baby had died presumed un-baptized, but because she still would not say who had been father of it. It was certain she would not say, not for coaxing, not for threat. Even grandmother she had not told; but grandmother knew. She had cried out loud that sunny day in summer when Catrine had ventured near the doorway with the child to get the warmth of the sun, and she Mor had asked the question, 'Who is he like? I have seen someone –'

Grandmother had flown into a terrible passion, she had sent Mor reeling with a blow on to the hard mud floor, and she had thrust Catrine and the baby back into the gloom. The child had been like his father, and who-ever that might be, she knew and did not like him. But even she would not say to others who he was.

As if it mattered! Why should a babe need any father at all?

It would have been pleasant to look after it, wash it and dress it, a living manikin. But here was one, too small and only pretence, but better than none at all. She had found it, mysteriously made, mysteriously left between the boulders of the burn for her. The water had softened its feet so that the clay was blurred there. But she would shape them again, and set the little bodach in the sun to dry.

But, what a hateful thing! The poor bodach was stuck full of pins. In its back and in its front, in its arms and legs and in its head, the tops of pins appeared. She sat quiet enough to please any fisher and busied herself pulling them out one by one.

There! They were all out. Just a bit of drying now in sun and wind. Lachlan had moved off downstream, she could sit and wait. As she sat she dreamed: how would she clothe him? Her gown was very torn, grandmother would not observe it if she tore a strip off the hem. She could wrap her bodachan up in that. But some day, today or tomorrow, she might ask Catrine if she still had the neckerchief that glinted like silk. Catrine never could go out now, she could not wear it; the beautiful thing of red and gold lay dull in the dark. It would make grand clothing for the bodachan, as grand as any in Castlehill.

She could no longer endure her delight without sharing it. She ran to her brother. 'Look what I found!' She held the bodachan out to him. There was still one pin stuck in its head and she gently drew it out. 'I found this in the water.'

But Lachlan sprang away as if he had been stung. His face grew pale under its sunspots. 'Take care! Drop it.'

She said, 'Why? It's only a little bodach.'

'Where did you find it?'

'In the burn, between two stones. See, the water has softened it, it would all have melted if I had not taken it out into the sun.'

'Quick, put it back. Don't stand there holding it in your hand, you little fool.'

'But why?'

Lachlan drew in his breath, as if to gain patience with

her. 'Because it is not a good thing. It is bad, very bad. Dangerous. Forbidden. Put it back where you found it and wash your hands in the running water upstream.'

'I am keeping it,' she said, and faced him with her chin up. 'I found it, and it is mine. I am keeping it.'

He would have struck her had he not been afraid to touch her holding it. He would not even walk home in her company. 'You'll get us all into fine trouble!' he called after her, raging.

She went home by herself with the bodachan in the breast of her gown.

Trouble? No. The next was a lucky day. They went to the Big House, ever hopeful, and this time when the doctor came out with Castlehill they were as joco as the day before they had been glum.

'I am beginning to have good hope of him,' the doctor was saying. 'See that he takes the potion, and let him keep the hare's foot always about him.'

'It is a miracle, a miracle!' answered Castlehill, reverently like a holy man. 'His mother would not believe it when yesterday he fell into an easy sleep. When he awoke he asked for food and took a little. And the skin seems clearer.'

The doctor mounted and rode away. The laird's eyes lit on Lachlan. 'Here, my hero!' said he. 'Take this and fill that little belly of yours.'

It was a penny. Solid in the hand, heavy. Six bodles all in one. It was too great to spend it by himself. Lachlan ran home, Mor at his heels, and ducked his head to the doorway, and eager, breathless, thrust the coin into his grandmother's hand.

She stood staring at it.

Before he could stop her, Mor told the story. 'He got it from the laird, from Castlehill. The young Master is

59

better today. We heard the doctor say he had good hope of him. That is why the laird was bountiful.'

The old woman had been looking at them. She looked once more at the coin. Her lips curled back as a dog's will. She hurled the coin clean out of the doorway, it fell among the whins, lost for ever. From her trembling mouth Gaelic curses came.

Catrine had looked up when she heard the name of Castlehill. She cried, 'No, no, no!' and covered her ears.

'Spare your tears,' the old woman said. 'I have put this word on them: they will never comb a grey head among the Cuthberts of Castlehill.'

She had made a meal ready, a dish of sowans with buttermilk, and a fragment of bannock. The children ate ravenously. But their grandmother left them at it, and went as quickly as she could down the slope of the hill.

Lachlan did not take long to finish his supper. In a moment or two he was out of the house and running down after her. Hidden by a hawthorn tree he watched her go to the burn, plodding along the bank to the place where he and Mor had been. Again he ran, this time to the alders by the water's edge, and he saw her wade into the burn, caution forgotten, without skirt raised. She stooped over the place where the boulders were, the very place from which his sister had taken the bodachan.

So, it was she, as he had feared. He knew what she had been about, the practice he had heard preached against at the town cross, the practice that came even under the censure of the Law. He guessed whom her art was aimed at. He was back in the house when, angry and cast down, she returned. As she spread the plaids upon the piles of heather that formed their beds, she muttered peevishly to herself. Mor fell asleep soon, her cheek on her hand, her hair spread round her. But Lachlan lay long awake. He was beset by fears and perplexities.

Should they confess to their grandmother that the – he could not say even to himself the name of the thing of horror that the bodachan was – that it was out in the air, freed from danger of melting, freed from torment of pins? Even should they brave her anger, what would be the good? She would set about making another, endangering herself and her family all over again. And how dared they tell her? He pictured, trembling, her dark brows. Surely she would not harm her grandchildren? Yet he knew that her wronged daughter was dearer to her than anything else in the world, even the children of her dead son. He could not tell her, his lips were held as if in a vice.

But, terrible to think of, she might know of it herself. Already the Master's recovery had roused her suspicions that her spell was failing. She had looked in the burn and found the thing gone. She must know it could not so soon have melted away, she must know it had been removed. Even if little Mor did not prattle the truth, might not one so potent divine who the culprits were? Would it not be safer to tell her outright?

This way and that his poor mind went. The household was stirring before he had well fallen asleep.

He called Mor from her task of feeding the hens. 'You must go straightway and put that bodachan back into the burn. You must take care to place it between the same two stones, where the water as it flows may melt it away. Why did you ever take it out at all? You should not have seen it, or seeing it you should have left it alone.'

She wept, fondling the little blunted image in her gown. 'I had to lift him out. He was naked and cold. He is my baby and I must cherish him.' For all her tears her face had a resolute look.

'Your baby! Do you not know what it is? You must put it back where you found it.'

She broke from his grasp. 'I cannot bear to. You do it, it is you who wish it.'

He threatened her with his fist. 'Do as I say!'

So she stripped it of the rags she had wrapped round it; naked again, poor bodachan, so forlorn! Her tears blinded her, she went clumsily along the burnside, Lachlan following her from the height of the field above. 'See and make it as it was. Put the pins back into it.'

She looked angrily up at him. 'No. I can't do that. They are lost.'

'But they are his bad deeds, he must die in the guilt of them.' And when she seemed bewildered, he shouted. 'Why did you go and meddle with it? Put them back in.'

'They are lost, I tell you. Besides, I would not even if I could.'

Watched by her brother's eye she waded into the pool, holding her bodachan. When she reached the two boulders that narrowed the burn to make a swift current, she sighed once then wedged the little thing between. She stood up to her knees in the cold and watched the rippling water wash over it. She could not bear to watch its mutilation; quickly she climbed the bank again and sat weeping, heedless of her brother's rough comforting. He left her to it, and ran off to try his luck somewhere. She sat mourning her lost baby and Catrine's lost baby, as if the two had become one.

Then, as if thought of the dead child had had power to summon his mother, Catrine appeared. She was pallid, as a blade of grass is pallid when it has lain beneath a stone out of the light, and she tottered as she walked like an old woman. Mor watched her warily as slowly she came.

Catrine came on patiently, until she stood above where Mor was sitting. Her reflection wavered on the pool. Mor feared to look again directly at her, as if she had been a ghost.

'Tell me, do you know – have you seen anywhere –' Her voice was like a rusty tool, she had spoken so little for so long. It faltered and ceased. But Mor knew what she meant. It was the bodachan she was after. She would take it out of the burn, but not to cherish it, to destroy it. Sure enough she went on, 'I fear she may have practised – and I must find it – for he, he – it might do him harm. Maybe it is that that already – Tell me if you have found her *corp creibhe*.' Naming the thing she shuddered. And Mor too was afraid. But she shook her head.

Then Catrine heaved a long sigh. 'You don't understand what I mean. How should you, but five years old, know of such things? Where's your brother? Where's Lachie?'

Mor gestured downstream. Slowly still, patiently, the older girl made her way along the bank, and Mor followed her, mistrustful. They had reached the place where the bank rose to join the pasture when they caught sight of Lachlan. He stood at the side of the highway, hoping for something from a passing traveller. He was so intent watching that he did not observe them till they were near.

When he heard Catrine's voice he wheeled round and stared at her aghast. 'Why have you left the house? It is not dark yet, you will be seen!' Angry with terror he flung himself upon her. 'You should not have come out after us, you will be our ruin. We are safe but for you.'

'I came to find – I must find –' He would not let her finish.

'You know well enough you must not be seen.'

Suddenly Mor cried out, 'Hide! I hear horses coming. Catrine, hide!'

The two younger children darted into cover behind a

clump of whin, but Catrine could not hasten; she was left standing alone beside the highway.

And the riders came up. One stopped alongside her. Lachlan put his hand over Mor's mouth to cut off her scream. For from behind their thorny cover they saw it was the Master. They had not seen him since his return from over the sea. How strange he looked! The brilliance of his plumed hat mocked his wan blemished face; the hand he put up to shade his eyes was wasted and trembled. For moments on end he sat there in his saddle motionless, gazing down on Catrine. His two servants reined in and came back to him; they spoke to him, but he sat heedless, gazing down on Catrine, motionless as a man turned into stone.

A servant at last leant over and touched the Master's horse, and the three rode on their way. He had to catch the reins, for the Master let them slip from his fingers; he had turned himself in the saddle, gazing back to where Catrine stood as if he was bewitched and could not draw his eyes away.

There was time to get Catrine home and tell grandmother, who might be able to form a wise plan for her escape. With Mor at his heels Lachlan made for the girl who was standing still as a rabbit spellbound by the weasel's eye. She looked as if she never again would stir from where she stood gazing. And he was filled with fury at her. 'This is your fault!' he cried, shaking her with all his might. 'You should not have left the house in daylight. You will get us all into danger. I wish you had never come back at all.'

Slowly she turned to him. He was astonished at her face. For it held no fear, no anger, no hate, only a look he had seen rarely enough in his rough life, the look of pitying love she had had when she sat dandling her baby before the men came and frightened her away.

No untoward event troubled the next day. Their grandmother had made two pence and there was food to eat.
Mor would have thought life good, had it not been for
her sorrow that by now the bodachan must be all melted
away.

But they were terrified early the day after when the
sound of horse hoofs sounded in their Millburn valley,
horse hoofs and a hubbub of voices. Along the track by
the cottages came a crowd: the children, outside the
door where they were scouring the pots, looked up in
dread, Mor clutching their grandmother's drab skirts.
Riders here! They saw the black horse of Castlehill;
with him were two magistrates and the minister of the
First Charge of the town. Ah, what should bring such
here? What but investigation, discovery, retribution!
This was the dreaded day. The secret was out. The
unlawful presence of Catrine had been made known to
the authorities if not by the Master then by their
neighbours clyping. Country folk, neighbours, ran
alongside the cavalcade. Who is so busy but he cannot
stop to see the taking of a harlot? Human nature, even
when not vicious, is greedy for sensation; to see others
in trouble serves to point one's own freedom from it.
The lips of the old woman muttered a curse on them
one and all.

When Lachlan heard the mumble of her speech he
knew terror sharper than any that had gone before. Not
only Catrine but the old woman herself was in peril.
Perhaps it was less Catrine and her unfathered babe
that had drawn judgement down than the old woman
and her making of the *corp creibhe*. He feared for himself
and for Mor: even supposing the old woman could with-
stand the Question, there might be that last and direst
torment of all, the tormenting before the eyes of the
accused of her family.

Surely that was it. For among the men who were coming he saw the Master. Pale, very pale, fearfully sick, like death. They had brought him here to confront the woman with her victim. Not only the taking of a harlot then, but the taking of a witch!

Castlehill and the magistrates dismounted. The minister, helped from his horse by a groom, in his turn helped the Master down. The young man was so weak he could not stand unaided; his father and the minister supported him. With their aid he tottered the few steps to the doorway. He stood and called in a weak wandering voice, 'Catrine! Catrine!'

And as if it had been loud as a trumpet Catrine came; thrusting aside her mother she stood gazing at the Master with that look on her face. He slipped from his helpers' hands and stumbled towards her. She stepped towards him and for a moment his support came from her arms alone.

'Young woman,' the minister said. 'Catrine, is this the man who was father to your babe?'

She spoke only to the Master, 'We had no shelter, he and I. He died of the cold.'

'You, sir, do you acknowledge her child?' the minister asked the Master then; and he bowed his head in affirmation. Husbanding his breath he spoke only to Catrine. 'They told me you were dead. But then I saw you. Forgive me! Oh forgive me, for I am going where I dare not carry my sins. So many! – I got this sickness in the Low Countries. I am myself the author of it, no one else, only I.'

They lifted him half fainting on to his horse, a groom walking beside him held him in the saddle. Long after her mother and the children were safely indoors, Catrine stood in the doorway looking after him.

It was not long after, a matter of days, when news spread among the little houses that the Master of Castlehill was dead.

On the third day after Lachlan was at the Big House door. From there he could hear the tolling of the High Kirk bell. He had not made it his business to follow after the procession, all black velvet and sable plumes, but he held his place against the other children to get any crumb that might fall his way from the funeral feast.

He was amazed when Murroch Og beckoned him to the back door, and loaded him with meat and game, cakes and comfits. 'Take it, *laoghain*! If it is the first, it will not be the last they send you.' He sent him secretly out by a side gate, else he should not have got very far with them. It was better than the times when Catrine came home to them from the Castle.

He did not know whether to go home with his spoils. His grandmother looked dark still, obdurate in hate against all the kindred of Castlehill. He dared not show her their gift.

As for Catrine, she had scarcely taken bite or sup since the Master's death. She moved everywhere as if in a dream, smiling.

Only Mor, he thought, would consent to share his feast. He hid the things among the whins and went looking for his sister. He found her beside the burn. Her drooped head rested on her hand. She was gazing into the water which by now had washed every particle of her bodachan away.

GREATER LOVE

Iain Crichton Smith

He wore a ghostly white moustache and looked like a
major in the First World War, which is exactly what he
had been. On our way to school – he being close to
retiring age – he would tell me stories about the First
World War and the Second World War, for he had been
in both. As we were passing the chemist's shop he would
be describing Passchaendale, walking along stiff and
erect, his eyes glittering behind his glasses.

'And there I was crouched in this trench, with my
water bottle empty. I had somehow or another survived.
All my good boys were dead, some up to their chests in
mud. The Jerries had got hold of our plan of attack, you
see. What was I to do? I had to wait all night, that was
clear. When the sun was just going down, I crawled
along the trench, and then across No Man's Land. I met
a Jerry and the struggle was fast and furious. I am afraid
I had to use the bayonet, or cold steel as we called it. But
the worst was not over yet, for one of our own sentries
fired on me. But I eventually managed to give him the
password. After that I was all right.'

He would pause and then as we passed the iron-
monger's he would start on another story. He taught
chemistry in the school and instead of telling his pupils
about solutions, or whatever they do in chemistry, he
would spend his time talking about the Somme or the
Marne. He spoke more about the First World War than
he did about the Second.

Once at the school party there was a quarrel between

him and the head of the French Department, who had also been in the First World War and who believed that he had won it. He questioned a statement which Morrison had made. It was, I think, a question of a date and they grew more and more angry and wouldn't speak to each other after that for a year or more. As I quite like both of them, it was difficult to know whose side to take.

The Headmaster didn't know what to do with him for parents came to the school continually to complain about his lessons – which as I have said consisted almost exclusively of accounts of his adventures in France and Flanders. The extraordinary thing was that he never repeated a story: all his tales were realistic and detailed and one could almost believe that they had happened to him. Either they had been experienced by him or they formed part of a huge mythology of legends which he had memorized, but which belonged to others. I was then Deputy Head of the school and it was my duty to see the parents and listen to their complaints.

'He will soon be retiring,' I would tell them soothingly. 'And he has been a good teacher in his time.'

And they would answer, 'That's all very well, but our children's education is being ruined. When are you going to speak to him?'

I did in fact try to speak to him a few times, but before I could do that he was telling me another of his stories and I found somehow or another that there was no way in which I could introduce my complaint to him.

'There was an angel, you know, at Mons, and I saw it. It was early morning and we were going over the top and we saw this figure bending over us from the sky. I thought it must have been an effect of the sun but it wasn't that. It was as if it was blessing us. We had our bayonets out and the light was flashing from them. I was in charge of a company at the time, the Colonel having been killed.'

69

This time I was so interested I said to him, 'Are you sure that it was an angel? After all, the rays of the sun streaming down and you, I presume being in an excited frame of mind . . .'

'No,' he said, 'it wasn't that . . . It was definitely an angel. I am quite sure of that. I could actually see its eyes.' And he turned to me. 'They were so compassionate. You have no idea what they looked like. You would never forget them.'

In those days we had lines and the pupils would assemble in the quadrangle in front of the main door and Morrison loved the little military drill so much that we gave him the duty most of the time. He would make them dress, keeping two paces between files, and they would march into the school in an orderly manner.

A young bearded teacher called Cummings who was always bringing educational books into the staffroom didn't like this militarism at all. One day he said to me, 'He's teaching them to be soldiers. He should be stopped.'

'How old are you?' I asked him.

'Twenty-two. What's that to do with it?'

'Twenty-two?' I said. 'Run along and teach your pupils English.' He didn't like it but I didn't want to explain to him why his age was important: he wouldn't have understood in any case. Still I couldn't find a way of speaking to Morrison without offending him.

'You'll just have to come straight out with it,' my wife said.

'No,' I said.

'What else can you do?'

'I don't know,' I said.

I was very conscious of the fact that I was considerably younger than Morrison. One day I said to him, 'How do you see your pupils?'

'What do you mean?'

'How do you see them?' I repeated.

'See them?' he said. 'They are too young to fight. But I see them as ready for it. Soon they will be taken.'

'Taken?'

'Yes,' he said. 'Just as we were taken.'

After a silence he said, 'One or two of them would make good officers. It's the gas that's the worst.'

'Have you told them about the gas?' I said, seizing on a tenuous connection between the First World War and chemistry.

'No,' he said, 'it was horrifying.'

'Well,' I said. 'Explain to them about the gas. Why don't you do that?'

'We never used it,' he said. 'The Jerries tried to use it, but the wind blew it back against them.' However, he promised that he would explain about the gas. I was happy that I had found a method of getting him to teach something of his subject, and tried to think of other connections. But I couldn't think of any more.

One day he came to see me, and said, 'A parent called on me today.'

'Called on you!' I said angrily. 'He should have come through me.'

'I know,' he said. 'He came directly to me. He complained that I was an inefficient teacher. Do you think I'm an inefficient teacher?'

'No,' I said.

'I have to warn them, you see,' he said earnestly. 'But I suppose I had better teach them chemistry after all.'

From that time onwards he became more and more melancholy and lost-looking.

He drifted through the corridors with his white ghostly moustache as if he was looking for a battle to take part in. Then he stopped coming to the staffroom and stayed in his classroom all the time. There were another three months to go before his retirement and if he carried on in this way I know that he would fade away and die. Parents ceased to come and see me about him and I was worried.

One day I called the best chemistry student in the school – Harrison – to my room and said, 'How is Mr Morrison these days?'

Harrison paused for a moment and then he said, 'He's very absent-minded, sir.' We looked at each other meaningfully, he tall and handsome in his blue uniform with the blue braid at the cuffs of his jacket. I fancied for a moment that I saw a ghostly white moustache flowering at his lips.

'I see,' I said, fiddling with a pen which was lying on top of the red blotting paper which in turn was stained with drops of ink like flak. 'How are you managing, the members of the class I mean?'

'We'll be all right,' said Harrison. Though nothing had been said between us he knew what I was talking about.

'I'll leave you to deal with it then,' I said.

The following day Morrison came gleefully to see me. 'An extraordinary thing happened to me,' he said. 'Do you know that boy Harrison? He is very brilliant of course and will go on to university. He asked me about the First World War. He was very interested. I think he will make a good officer.'

'Oh,' I said.

'He has a fine mind. His questions were very searching.'

'I see,' I said, doodling furiously.

'I cannot disguise the fact that I was unhappy here for a while. I was thinking: here they are and I am unable to warn them of what is going to happen to them. You see, no one told us that there were going to be two world wars. I was in the sixth year when the First World War broke out. I was studying chemistry just like Harrison. They told us we would be home for Christmas. Then after I came back from the war I did chemistry in university. I forgot about the war and then the second one came along. By that time I was teaching here, as you know.'

'Yes,' I said.

'In the First World War I was so young. Everyone was so ignorant and naive. No one told us anything. We were very enthusiastic, you see. You recollect of course that there hadn't really been a big war since the Napoleonic Wars. Naturally there had been the Boer War and the Crimean War, but these had been side issues.'

'Of course,' I said.

'You were in the Second World War yourself,' he said. 'So you will know.'

But as I had been in the Air Force that didn't in his opinion count. And yet I too had seen scarves of flame like those of students streaming from planes as they exploded in the sky. I felt the responsibility of my job intensely, and though I was younger I felt the older of the two. I felt protective towards him as if it was I who was the officer and he the young starry-eyed recruit.

After Harrison had asked him his questions Morrison was quite happy again and could return to the First World War with a clear conscience. Then one day a parent came to see me. It was in fact Major Beith, a red-faced man with a fierce bristling moustache who had been an officer in the Second World War.

'What the bloody hell is going on?' he asked me. 'My son isn't learning any chemistry. Have you seen his report card? It's bloody awful.'

'He doesn't work,' I said firmly.

73

'I'm not saying that he's the best worker in the world. The bugger watches TV all the time. But that's not the whole explanation. He's not being taught. He got fifteen per cent for his chemistry.'

I was silent for a while and then I said, 'Education is a very strange thing.'

'What?' And he glared at me from below his bushy eyebrows.

I leaned towards him and said, 'What do you think education consists of?'

'Consists of? I send my son to the school to be taught. That's what education consists of. But the little bugger tells me that all he learns about is the Battle of the Marne.'

'Yes,' I said. 'I appreciate that. But on the other hand I sometimes think that . . .' I paused. 'He sees them, I don't know how he sees them. He sees them as the Flowers of Flanders. Can you believe that?'

His bulbous eyes raked me as if with machine gunfire.

'I don't know what you're talking about.'

I sighed. 'Perhaps not. He sees them as potential officers, and NCOs and privates. He is trying to warn them. He is trying to tell them what it is like. He loves them, you see,' I said simply.

'Loves them?'

'That's right. He is their commanding officer. He is preparing them.' And then I said daringly, 'What's chemistry in comparison with that?'

He looked at me in amazement. 'Do you know,' he said, 'that I am on the Education Committee?'

'Yes,' I said staring him full in the eye.

'And you're supposed to be in charge of discipline here?'

'I am,' I said. 'I have to think of everything. Teachers have rights too.'

'What do you mean, teachers have rights.'

'Exactly what I said. If pupils have rights so too have teachers. And one cannot legislate for love. He loves them more than you or I are capable of loving. He sees the horror waiting for them. To him chemistry is irrelevant.'

For the first time I saw a gleam of understanding passing across the cloudless sky of his eyes. About to get up, he sat down again, smoothing his kilt.

'It's an unusual situation,' I said, 'and by the nature of things it will not last long. The fact is that we don't know the horrors in that man's mind. Every day he is there he sees the class being charged by bayonets. He sees Germans in grey helmets. He smells the gas seeping into the room. He is protecting them. All he has to save them is his stories.'

'You think?' he said, looking at me shrewdly.

'I do,' I said.

'I see,' he said, in his crisp military manner.

'He is not like us,' I said. 'He is being destroyed by his imagination.' As a matter of fact I knew that the major's son was lazy and difficult and that part of the reason for that was the affair that his father was conducting with a married woman from the same village.

He thought for a while and then he said, 'He has only two or three months to go. We can last it out.'

'I knew you would understand,' I said.

He shook his head in a puzzled manner and then he left the room.

The day before he was to retire Morrison came to see me. 'They are as prepared as I can make them,' he said. 'There is nothing more I can do for them.'

'You've done very well,' I said.

'I have tried my best,' he said. 'Question and answer,' he said. 'I should have done it in that way from the beginning. Start from the known and work out to the

75

unknown. But they didn't know enough so I had to start with the unknown.'

'There was no other way,' I said.

'Thank you,' he said courteously. And he leaned across the desk and shook me by the hand.

I said that I hoped he would enjoy his retirement, but he didn't answer.

'Goodbye for the present,' I said. 'I'm afraid I shall have to be away tomorrow. A meeting, you understand.' His eyes clouded for a moment and then he said, 'Well, goodbye then.'

I thought for one terrible moment that he would salute me, but he didn't. As a matter of fact I didn't see him often after his retirement. It was time that chemistry was taught properly. Later, however, I heard that he had lost his memory and couldn't tell his stories of the First World War any more. I felt this as an icy bouquet on my tongue, but the slate had to be cleaned, education had to begin again.

SHORE DANCES

George Mackay Brown

We are in serious trouble, here in the island.

They are in serious trouble, though they never had more coins to rattle in their pouches and to kist under the beds.

We are in serious trouble. Mr Sweyn the laird has been, and gone again, purple-faced with wrath, to Kirkwall, to report to the authorities there. No doubt he will try to do his best for the islanders, and turn away wrath from their doors. But he cannot prevent the mockery that will fall about his own head.

The island woke at dawn, a week ago exactly, to see a three-masted armed ship anchored out in the bay, and a small boat rowing between ship and shore, with three men in her.

There was anxiety until it could be known what the ship was, and what she wanted. It was unlikely to be either the Press Gang seeking recruits, or sheep thieves or smugglers; they went about their business in the dark of the moon.

The boat grounded. A young man stepped ashore.

The island men watched from behind rocks. Only Ran Eunson showed himself at the mouth of Rinians Cave: a huge powerful young man with fists like clubs and a voice like a trumpet. Ran hailed them.

What unutterably strange music was it that came from the sailor's mouth: a sweet strange incomprehensible jargon? Hands accompanied the voice, fluid lucent shapes in the air. Poor Ran gaped at him.

Fish – it was obvious that the graceful young man from the ship wanted fresh fish. He sculpted fish with both hands His right hand made undulations in the wind.

Ale – he drew a beautiful bottle shape in air, he tilted a cup, he made a small precise comical stagger on the wet stones.

Butter, cheese – he knew what went on in farms at milking time. He knew how churns are steered.

Water – when you think about it, it must be difficult to mime water. The sailor tilted his face skyward, he held out both hands. One could almost see the shine of rain, after a long drought, over cheekbone and knuckle; and his mouth imitated the gentle plangencies of water on grass and stone. And then, smiling, he pointed to the well above the shore. There was no doubt that the ship wanted water, and urgently.

Bread – he imitated a ploughman stumbling after an ox (the sea gleam on his face, notwithstanding). He imitated a scytheman. He broke a round of air in two and put a fragment of delicious nothingness into his mouth.

Honey – he wore a bee-mask, he flung red-hot seething sun embers from his face. He sucked from his fingers delicious drops.

Now that the peaceful intentions of the ship in the bay had been made obvious, the island men rose up from behind their rocks, one after the other, and showed themselves without fear. Also Bella Swann came down from the field where she had been milking her father's cow. And an old man, Sander Groat, came hirpling rapidly on a stick along the shore road, in case there might be some free tobacco going. And Merran came from the fishing bothy, shawled, working lips and gums: to see, maybe, one marvel yet before the last marvel.

Apart from everything else, it had been a rare enter-tainment to see the slow dance and mime; and to hear the beautiful incomprehensible music from the harp of the stranger's exquisitely moulded mouth.

(All this was told me, starkly, in my study at the Manse, by Saul the shepherd before noon. Saul had seen the complete performance from beginning to end. With-out Saul Birsa, Mr Sweyn and I would not know the half of what goes on here in the island.)

The young foreigner stood at last before them, all smiles and open palms. He had no more signs to make. Let there now be some kind of reply.

The island men drifted together. It was obvious what the ship wanted. The next urgent question to be answered was, what would the island receive in exchange for bread, water, ale, fish, honey, cheese and butter?

James Tomison was appointed to negotiate for them.

James Tomison stepped forward.

James Tomison made the action of opening a pouch and counting out a fistful of money: all urgent fingers and spread palm.

It was not such a fine mime as the young sailor's, by any means, but it was as effective in its way. James Tomison was only half through his reply when the stranger nodded eagerly, and laughed, and gestured to the sailor sitting in the stern.

That sailor brought from a belt hidden under his shirt a leather poke. He shook it; it rang like a bell. He loosened the thong. He poured a silver stream over the wet stones. The shore was possessed by myriad flashings, by the ringing of many small bells.

I regret to say that, at this point, an island man who shall be nameless proposed to rush on the three foreigners ·at once and overpower them, then gather up the silver scatterings and share it out in equal parts.

However, the majority of the island men are honourable.

Within an hour a considerable store of the island's natural bounty was stacked high on the shore. Many buckets came heavy and brimming from the well. (By this time a second larger longboat had left the ship, with a lashing of water-barrels in her.)

Until mid-morning, while the tide ebbed, the exchange went on: the loading of the boats, the picking of silver pieces large and small from rockpool and seaweed.

Never had the island men beheld such treasure. (In the sharing out, no doubt, there would be some trouble, a bloody nose and a thunder-laden eye here and there, and some small bitternesses that might outlinger the winter.)

Finally the loading was completed, the last ale-flagon stowed and the last water-barrel lashed down.

The young man, his face grave now, bowed in acknowledgement of a fair day's trading. The island men answered with flashings out of their beards.

Oars were fitted into rowlocks. The blades made fine little singing circles. Two men strained at the bow to push off.

The young foreigner lingered still. He drew from his waistcoat pocket a coin that far outshone those that had hitherto enriched the morning. Even Ran Eunson the stupid giant knew gold when he saw it. The solitary piece flashed back from the sun into two dozen eyes. Then the Frenchman lifted his forefinger and pointed straight at Bella Swann, who was standing there on the road above with her milk-bucket in her hand.

Again, I am sorry to say that two or three men (I will not mention names) would gladly have taken that golden coin and afterwards thrust Bella in among the honeycombs and lobsters in the longboat. But Jimmy Ardale was there, fortunately, and at once he pranced about and threatened to put a knife into any man who wanted to go on with that particular piece of marketing. He flashed his knife round at the foreigner. Poor Bella didn't know what it was all about. When she heard the shouts down by the cave-mouth, and saw the glint of Jimmy's knife, she gathered up her skirts and summer-smelling bucket and made for the milking-shed of Smelt: only once turning her comely face back. (All this Saul Birsa told me.)

At that smouldering and flash and outcry along the shore, the Frenchman didn't linger for another second. He made a sign. He vaulted lightly on board. With thew and oar-blade the longboats were thrust away from the stones and sand. A voice cried from the deck of the big ship. Voices answered from the two out-drifting boats. Laughter, made sweet and perilous on the harpstrings of the sea, passed between sailor and sailor.

'James Tomison, man,' I said in the kirk vestry later that afternoon, 'what were you thinking of, at all? You are a man of prudence and intelligence. Can it be you are not aware that the Kingdom of Great Britain and the Kingdom of France have been at war with one another since last March? I know not, James, what the end of this business will be. You have given aid and comfort to an enemy ship – no peaceful merchant either, for Saul tells me there was a line of black-mouthed guns along the hull of her. She was a fighting ship, James. That makes a difference, a very grave difference. James, technically you and all your fellow bargainers, that thought yourselves so smart this morning, may be traitors. I do not know – I am no lawyer. James, it may be you will need the bits of French silver to defend yourselves in the courts of admiralty. It is a bad business.

Mr Sweyn must be told, of course. Why, man, did you not send up to the Manse if you were in any doubts about the legality of your proceedings this morning? No, you were too blinded with the shining and the music of all that silver. Good day to you, James Tomison. I have nothing more to say just now. I will write a letter with a full account of this incident to Mr Sweyn in Kirkwall. I hope Mr Sweyn will be willing and able to speak up for you. I fear, however, there are in Kirkwall men more powerful than Mr Sweyn your protector.'

Then, seeing how blanched the face of the poor man was, and how his hands holding his bonnet trembled like waterdrops, I said, 'Now, James, it may be all right. I think it will be all right. You do not read newssheets, you live in simplicity and ignorance, at the very extreme of the kingdom. How should you know what nations are embattled, or what princes look coldly the one on the other? James, man, I will speak for you all to Mr Sweyn, and Mr Sweyn (I know it, though he will be troubled) will speak on your behalf to them that sit in seats of authority.

'After this, James, let all your dealings be with corn-stalks and peat and cod-fish.'

NO-MAN'S-LAND

Stephanie Markman

On the first day Connie feels nothing but numbness, beautiful, beautiful numbness. People – women – come and go, and Connie is dimly aware of them addressing her and, more surprisingly still, of replying to them. From time to time one of her children comes crying, tugging at her arm.

'They're hungry,' she hears herself saying at last to one of the women.

'There's a grocer's up the way, across the road and round to your left,' says the woman, Elaine, looking up briefly from her knitting.

Connie struggles into her raincoat and slopes out to the shops. Halfway there she remembers her children, left behind in the house, and dimly she wonders if they're all right.

'You can't just leave your kids running around like that,' reproves another of the women when she gets back. 'Why didn't you ask? You're supposed to ask one of us if you're leaving them here.' And Connie hears her voice come from somewhere far away, apologizing.

Later in the day she wanders into one of the bedrooms and picks up a mirror from the chest of drawers. She stares at the face in the mirror, traces its outline with her fingers, rubbing gently over the area where a large, purple bruise is reflected back at her. Like a magic colouring book, she thinks, smiling and wetting her finger and rubbing over the hard, silver surface.

'Here!' says a woman, coming briskly into the bedroom. 'What're you doing with my stuff? You nicked anything?' She wrenches the mirror away, shoves Connie firmly out of the room and slams the door.

'Never mind, love,' says the kindly woman in the hall. 'You come and sit down again. Upset you, did she?'

But Connie shakes her head, and allows herself to be led back into the living room, put back into a chair.

Malcolm, her youngest, comes running up, detaching himself from a communal children's squabble. 'When're we going home, Mum?' he says. 'It's dirty here.'

Connie tucks his tee-shirt in. 'Not just now, Malcolm,' she says, vague.

He punches her. 'Well I'm hungry, anyway,' he shouts angrily. 'You'd better have our supper ready soon.' He runs back to join the others.

'Here you are, love,' says the woman from the hall.

She puts a cup of tea into Connie's hand and Connie raises it, automatically, to her lips, scalding her mouth.

'Here, careful, that's hot,' says the woman. 'You are in a bad way, aren't you? Here,' she says, slipping her hand into her pocket, 'have one of these. I've got plenty to spare.' She hands her a blue-and-green capsule and Connie puts it obediently into her mouth. 'That'll make you feel calmer,' says the woman with some satisfaction.

Connie, already out at the outer limits of calmness, swallows the hard lump in her mouth, washing it down with the tea.

'That's right,' nods the woman. 'Soon be better. I remember when I first came here, the state I was in –'

Her voice rambles on in the background, rising and falling. What is she saying? Connie tries to concentrate, but the layers of cottonwool in her brain are encircling her, preventing her from thinking. She subsides into her chair, listens remotely.

On the morning of the second or the third day, Connie wakes early in the grey, whitewashed room, turns over sleepily to snuggle up to Jim, finds only a child's small, inert body and the wetness where the child has pissed the bed. 'Jim?' she says.

She gropes further over, encounters two more small, sleeping forms, lies back and stares at the ceiling.

Funny to wake next to someone every morning all these years and then, suddenly, not to. Must be funny for him, too. Or maybe he's already moved someone else in. Her mouth tightens. Off down the pub that first evening, chatting to the barmaid, probably: my wife's away, why don't you come round? And the woman, of course, jumping at it. Been eyeing him up since I don't know when. The cow.

Connie turns over on to her side, looks at the wall, wriggles away from the damp on the sheets. Nasty, nylon sheets they are, too. Wouldn't have them in my house. Get some cotton ones, said Jim, throwing a fiver at her. I'm not sleeping under those slimy things your mum gave us.

An altercation in the hall. Big, motherly Carol is running up and down, screeching. Connie hears doors opening and closing, huddles further down in the bed. Women run in and out of rooms, making phone calls, yelling.

'What is it, Mum?' Sharon stirs by her side.

'Nothing, love,' says Connie, pushing the sour-smelling child over towards the others. 'You go back to sleep.' Sharon turns over, snuggles into the blankets.

Jim, thinks Connie. If I find out you've had another woman there – but then, what's a man to do? He'll be wanting his meals, I left his clothes dirty, he'll be needing some company. Always said he could find something better than me.

The door bell rings and a woman runs to open it. 'What's going on then?' says a disembodied voice. Janie's voice.

'Oh, it's Carol,' says Rose, shuffling back down the hall. 'Woke me up, she did, carrying on –' The living room door closes on her words.

Connie sits slowly up, reaches over to light a cigarette. She sits on the edge of the bed, puts her slipperless feet gingerly down on the cold lino, puffs meditatively. Just let me find out he's had someone there, that's all. She wraps her raincoat around her, shivers, then goes to rummage in her handbag for a coin for the meter. Wait till the room's warm, then get the kids up. And hope to God that things've quietened down in the other room by then.

Evening. Connie jumps nervously to her feet at the sound of the key in the door. But it is only the women, returning from the pub. Carol goes straight off to bed.

'What happened this morning, with her, then?' asks Connie of Elaine.

'Oh, that woman who left here last night stole her bloody Librium, the cow,' says Elaine. 'Her acting too good for us and all. Just shows you, doesn't it?'

'We don't actually *know* it was Rosemary, Elaine.' Janie is trying to be fair. 'It's just an assumption.'

'I don't see what else you can bloody assume,' says Rose. 'We checked Carol's room, didn't we? Unless you think one of us took them.'

'Oh no, no, I wasn't suggesting that.' Janie looks crestfallen, embarrassed. 'I just thought we might be jumping to conclusions, that's all.' She takes herself off, muffled up in her duffle coat.

'Women's libber, that one,' says Elaine, nodding her head. 'You can always tell. Not that I mind, she's a nice enough girl, is Janie. Only she doesn't half push it down your throat sometimes.'

Rose, who has been out in the kitchen making coffee, comes back with a laden tray. 'You know what you could do with, Connie,' she says critically. 'I reckon you'd look really nice with a perm.'

'Really? Do you think so?' Connie is flattered by her interest. She pulls at her hair, giggles. 'Couldn't afford it though,' she says regretfully.

'Won't cost you a penny, love.' Rose hands her a cup, comes over to fiddle with her scalp. 'Used to be a hairdresser, I did, before I got married. My old man wouldn't hear of it, of course. "I'm not having a wife of mine working, now we're getting along in the world," says he. Took all the stuff with me when I left, didn't I? No time to get clothes, forgot my family allowance book, but I grabbed all my hairdressing stuff as I ran. I thought: well, maybe I'll need it now after all. So I'll do it for you tomorrow, eh?'

'I can't *pay* you, Rose. My S.S. money hasn't come through or anything.'

'Con, you'll have to learn to take things from people, you know,' says Elaine. 'Rose was offering to do it for nothing, weren't you, Rose?'

'For practice,' says Rose, grinning.

'And I'll look after the kids while you do it,' says Elaine. 'Who knows, maybe modom here can find fellers for all of us, once you've dolled her up a bit.'

They go off to bed, laughing.

But I don't want a feller, thinks Connie later. She pushes up against Malcolm, moves him over, snuggles down into the warm spot he has vacated. Enough trouble with the first one. Wonder what *he's* doing now? Maybe he's lying in bed too, all on his own, feeling lonely. Maybe he's missing me.

Her hand moves tentatively downwards, but she checks it, sighs, and turns over on her side. Dirty, that is. Just have to do without it from now on, that's all.

And then there, on the fourth day, is Jim. Connie sees him coming towards them down the street and her heart starts to judder with panic. Perhaps he hasn't seen them. Perhaps they can get away. But: 'Dad!' cries Philip in delight, and the three children rush towards him, yelling and waving. Connie follows on, nervous.

'Hello, Con,' he says, casual as you please. 'Done something to your hair, have you? Looks smashing. Must've cost you a bit, though. How're you keeping?'

'Didn't cost me anything, Jim,' she says. 'One of the women did it for me. And I'm fine,' she adds defiantly. 'Just fine.'

'I shouldn't let one of those lezzies touch you if I was you,' he says.

'You what?'

'You heard. I heard you were staying up at that place, that –'

'Refuge,' she supplies coldly.

'Yeah. Well they're all a bunch of lesbians up there. Common knowledge, that is. I hope you keep your room locked at night, I'd hate to think of them getting at you. Or at Sharon.' He strokes the child's head protectively.

'What, Dad?' says Sharon, looking up at him. 'What's that?'

'Never you mind,' says Connie hurriedly. 'You kids just go and look in that window over there. Decide what you want from Santa.' She packs them off, protesting.

'I want to talk to you, Con,' says Jim softly. 'You can't just go off like this, my mates all think I'm daft. I have to see you.'

'I can't, Jim.'

88

He moves closer. 'I miss you, you know. I don't know what you want to go running off like that for, no word, nothing. Look, I'll be on the corner with my van at ten o'clock. You just pop out and we'll chat for a few minutes. That's fair enough, isn't it?'

'I won't come, Jim,' she says, calling to the children. She pulls them away, almost running up the street.

'I want to say goodbye to Dad,' sobs Malcolm.

'We'll miss the bus,' says Connie fiercely. 'There's no time.'

And I won't go, she says to herself as they board the bus back. I won't, I won't.

Ten past ten. Connie walks quickly down the street to the familiar van on the corner. 'I can only stay a minute, mind,' she says, getting in.

'Oh Con, it's good to see you.' He puts his arms round her, kisses her. 'Remember what it was like before we were married, when we used to go courting in my car? Not as posh as this, was it? But it was good, eh?' His hand slips up under her skirt and begins to insinuate itself under the waistband of her tights. 'When're you coming back, then?'

She moves away. 'I'm not coming back, Jim. You'll be getting a letter, I expect.'

'A letter? What sort of a letter?'

'I'm applying for custody. They thought it was the best thing to do.'

'You're applying for what?' He turns slowly, ominously, in his seat, his face purpling. 'They thought it was the best thing, did they? We'll see about that.'

Connie feels his hands closing around her throat in a familiarly terrifying gesture. She struggles, chokes, tries to scream, bangs with her leg against the door of the van. Jim's hands tighten around her, crushing against her

Adam's apple, Jim's face is pressed right up against her, scarlet. She opens her mouth, gasps for air. The door is wrenched, suddenly, open.

'You let her go, you bastard.'

Connie hears Janie's voice coming from somewhere far away, hears the sound of running feet, hears the other women's voices in the background. 'I thought she'd be here,' says someone. They pull her away from his suddenly lax hands, pull her out of the van, slam the door. 'Fucking pig,' says Elaine, kicking the side.

'For God's sake, Elaine,' says Carol. 'Don't needle him. Just let him go.'

The van drives off. 'Come on, Connie,' says Elaine wearily. 'Let's get you back to the house. What the fuck did you want to go seeing him for? No sense, no sense at all.'

Janie arranges to meet Connie in town for lunch. I'll pay, she says. Christmas treat, sort of. Connie runs puffing up the hill, late, cigarette dangling from her mouth, trying as best she can to forget the frantic cries of her kids, left behind in the capable hands of Carol.

Janie, already in the cafe, looks at her reproachfully. 'It's self-service, Connie,' she says. 'Do you want to go and get yourself something? I went round while I was waiting.'

A fitting punishment. Have to pay for it myself, now, no doubt. Connie slams a plate of congealing food down on to her tray, moves grimly on down the line. But Janie, when she returns, wordlessly hands her a couple of pound notes, laughingly pushing away the change. 'Spend it on the kids,' she says. 'Get them some sweeties from me.'

Connie shovels the food into herself rapidly, then reaches with a sigh for her coffee, lighting up, at Janie's offer, a cigarette. Stuyvesant, it is. None of your Regals for Janie. She draws on it luxuriantly. 'Could get addicted to these if I'm not careful,' she says.

'Oh yes, they're nice, aren't they? Here, you have the rest of the packet. I ought to give them up, anyway.'

Janie pushes them over to her and Connie, startled, demurs. 'It's all right, honestly,' says Janie. 'I've got lots more money than you right now, haven't I?'

'You a communist?' asks Connie curiously.

'Yes, you could say that.' Hesitating. 'How are *you*, anyway? Settling in all right?'

'Oh yes.' Connie sucks doubtfully on her cigarette. Supposed to sing for her supper, obviously. 'Nice for the kids,' she offers, 'having all the others around.'

'Oh yes,' says Janie happily. 'I often think it's good for them, don't you, having other adults to relate to?'

'How do you mean?' says Connie, defensively.

'Oh, I was just thinking that . . . well, my own childhood . . .' Janie swallows, looks uncomfortable. 'I mean . . . we all had to just make do with our parents, not that they weren't fine, but . . . well, if they didn't have time for you, that was it, really. I live in a big house now, with lots of people, and I'm sure it's nicer for the children. More adults to choose from.'

'Commune, is it?' Connie twirls her fag end on the rim of the ashtray, moulding and shaping the ash.

'Uh-huh,' says Janie. 'You must come down some time, see it,' she says feebly.

'Mmmm,' says Connie politely, struggling to her feet.

'Oh, don't go yet.' Janie looks aghast, tugs her, reluctantly, back down. 'I wanted to ask you how things are, how you're feeling. Part of my job, you know.' The last said with a flourish of self-mockery. She reaches without thinking for a cigarette, recoils with a start. 'Might I have one of your cigarettes, Connie?'

Connie grins, relaxing a little. 'Go on, you daft thing,' she says, pushing the packet back towards her. 'And I'll get you a coffee,' she adds, moving purposefully away before Janie can intercept her.

They lean back in their chairs, try to blow smoke rings, giggle. 'How old were you when you got married?' asks Janie suddenly.

'Seventeen,' says Connie, stiffening.

'Why?'

'How d'you mean, why?' Connie tenses again. 'I was pregnant, that's why.' She draws her raincoat around her, bristling.

'Oh Connie,' says Janie. 'I'm sorry, I didn't mean to offend you. I was just interested, that's all.'

She lays her hand clumsily on Connie's sleeve but Connie shoves it away. 'And I don't want the fags, either, thanks,' she says, turning to go. From the corner of her eye she sees Janie slump back in her chair, defeated. Just interested, was she? Interfering, more like.

'I'll see you then, Janie,' she says, escaping from the table. She hurries to the escalator and down out of sight.

And even if she wasn't, even if she was just being . . . well, I don't need her charity, bloody right I don't.

Coming back slowly from the bus, squelching over the grass, she looks up to see the children hurtling towards her. When Philip reaches her it is not an embrace he offers but an envelope, grubby and dog-eared from too much handling.

'It's from Dad!' he shouts.

Connie stares stricken at the familiar scrawl, turning it over to gaze, her stomach lurching, at the huge letters, SWALK, emblazoned across the flap. She colours, thrusts the envelope into her coat pocket.

'Read it now, Mum,' says Sharon.

'Yes, go on, Mum, we want to see it, Mum.'

'I'll thump you, Philip,' says Connie severely. 'It's none of your business, none of you. Now get back to the house, right now.' She raises her hand and they grudgingly comply.

'Can we see it later, though, Mum?' says Sharon hopefully. But Connie doesn't hear, doesn't reply. 'Here, Mum,' says Sharon, persevering.

'Mmmm?'

'We rushed and got it as soon as the postman came, we didn't let any of them others see it.'

'Eh?' says Connie. 'Oh, good.'

Clever kid. It wouldn't do, after all, for anyone to know about it. Especially with that message on the back. Daft bugger, her Jim. She smiles faintly, pushes the door to her room and drops the coat on the bed. For later.

On the seventh day Rose and Elaine have a fight. Connie sits in the midst of the chaos in the living room, trying to sink away to nothing, to remain invisible. 'I don't like this, Mum,' whines Malcolm.

'Shhhh,' says Connie, invisible Connie. 'It'll be over in a minute.'

'Will it fuck,' says Rose. She turns back accusingly to her adversary across the room. 'And another thing,' she says. 'Two tins of spaghetti, I had, in the cupboard, and there's neither sight nor sound of them now. Where've *they* gone, I'd like to know?'

'I haven't touched your bloody spaghetti. Wouldn't feed it to pigs.' Elaine is bristling with fury, stalking round in the corner. 'Proper food, I feed my kids, not that tinned shit. *And* I wash the pans when I've finished with them. Unlike madam muck here –'

'Oh, very nice. Very nice. And who was it, I'd like to

know, told someone else to put their feet up last Sunday and did all their washing up too? *And* made a cup of tea after? While some other ilk time was sitting about watching the telly?'

'Idle cow?' says Elaine, advancing to the middle of the room. She rolls her sleeves up purposefully. 'Who're you calling a cow?'

Connie clutches Malcolm's damp, sticky paw, sidles out of the room and makes a bolt for her own. Slumping on the bed she reaches into her pocket for Jim's letter. The second one, this is. Pages and pages of romantic nonsense, fond recollections of better times and even, at the end, a poem. He's lonely, is Jim. Can't do without her. Missing the kids, too. And oh, Con, everything'll be different this time if you just come back. Give us another chance. Your affectionate etc. And all the old excuses, all the old reasons why things went wrong in the past, why they wouldn't do again. And here am I, thinks Connie grimly, supposedly enjoying all this peace and quiet away from it, trying to start off again. And just listen to it, a real home from home.

A tap on the door. 'Mum,' says Sharon importantly, 'it's the phone. It's for you.'

'Who is it?' says Connie.

'It's . . . Dad,' squeaks Sharon, preparing to run. But Connie grabs her, pulls her into the room. 'How the hell did he get my number?' she hisses. 'Unlisted, this phone is.'

'I don't know, Mum,' says Sharon, pulling away.

'I'll ask him. I'll ask him where he got it.'

'It wasn't me, Mum, honest. Phil gave it him.'

'When did Philip see him?' asks Connie, disbelieving.

'Out . . . outside. When we play. He comes to see us, does Dad, brings us sweets and things. Don't tell him, will you, Mum. He'll kill us.'

'You rotten little liar,' says Connie. 'You wait till I get off the phone. You and your brothers. I'll give you what for.'

She marches out to the living room, past the now-silent women, reaches for the phone. 'If you wouldn't mind,' she says to them, 'I'd like a bit of privacy. Personal call, this is. My . . . mother.' They nod understandingly, file out.

'Here, Rose.' Elaine's voice comes muffled from the hallway. 'Got that knitting pattern, have you?'

They disappear into her room.

And on the tenth day Carol goes home.

'Ran out of Librium, I expect, poor old cow,' says Rose dispassionately as she fills the teapot.

'Janie won't like it,' says Elaine, staring out of the window. 'Takes it very hard, she does. Bags I don't have to tell her. How about you, Con? Thick as thieves, you two.'

She breathes on the window, doodling with her finger on the steamy patch.

'I'd . . . rather not,' says Connie.

Elaine swings round to look at her. 'Had a quarrel?'

'Oh, no,' says Connie airily. 'I'd just . . . rather not. How about Nicola? She's the new girl now. You know what Janie said, she said we were to encourage her, get her to do things.'

'Yeah, that'll teach her to sit in her room, eh?' says Rose.

'You and Janie not getting on, then, Con?' says Elaine persistently. 'Bit of a pain, isn't she?'

'Oh, Janie's all right,' says Connie uncomfortably.

'Oh, she means well, does Janie,' says Rose. 'Got a good heart. Just goes a bit overboard, that's all. I bet she'd've been dead upset if she'd've known about that bloke I was going out with the other week, anyway, eh Elaine? Out of the frying pan into the fire, she'd've said.'

'Well, she'd've been right for once, wouldn't she? He was a right pig, that bloke, Con. Threatened to hit her if she stopped seeing him.'

'Ach, they're all the same, men,' says Connie with some disgust.

'You sound like Janie,' says Elaine, laughing.

'No, no,' says Connie, 'it was just . . . just . . . a manner of speaking. I don't . . . *hate* . . . men. I don't even hate Jim any more.'

'You want to be careful, Con. You'll be back with him before you know where you are.'

'Oh no, I wouldn't go back,' says Connie. 'Only . . . you do *miss* them, sometimes, don't you? Someone to cuddle up to at night.'

'And someone to belt you in the morning.'

'Yes, but,' says Connie, 'don't you think they might change? If they were really missing you, I mean.'

The others hoot derisively. 'Yes, and pigs might fly,' says Elaine, getting up to take the tea things through. 'You wouldn't catch me going back, Con, not if my life depended on it.'

But two days later, when Connie gets up to light the living room fire, she finds a note on the mantelpiece. Elaine, too, has gone home.

'Bit dismal here, isn't it?' says Janie.

They are sitting in the basement of the housing department, in a long, dingy, grey and green room with black plastic seating along the walls and imitation-wood coffee tables scattered with dog-eared magazines. Connie sighs and looks around for Malcolm.

'D'you know who you're going to see, Connie?' Janie

enquires. Connie hands her the slip of pink paper she was given on arrival.

'Oh dear,' says Janie. 'Mrs Brown.'

'Who's she?'

Janie points to a tall, angular woman stalking through the doorway. Grey hair rigidly backcombed into shape, gold-rimmed glasses, a clipboard in one hand.

'Your local friendly Gestapo agent,' she says. She pats Connie's hand. 'Go on, you'll be all right. Stiff upper lip and all that. I'll keep Malcolm out here, shall I?'

Connie nods gratefully as the woman in the doorway signals her to come in.

'Mrs Munroe? This way, please.'

'Now, Mrs Munroe. How long have you been married? And where did you live all that time?'

Mrs Brown fixes Connie with a piercing stare, her pencil hovering over the clipboard. Connie feels faint with alarm. She gazes round the interview room – the same green and grey walls, the straight-backed chairs, the plain metal desk – as if seeking inspiration. Her eyes focus on a large map of the city, pink and blue and yellow and green and orange like old school atlases.

'Nine and a half years,' she says finally. 'And oh, we lived in Coventry at first, and then we moved here – oh, seven and a bit years ago, it must be. To the house in Sheldon Drive, the same one.'

'Children?' says Mrs Brown, leaning forward to imprison every word.

'Three.'

'Three?' says Mrs Brown, making a note. 'Dear me, Mrs Munroe, you couldn't have disliked your husband all *that* much, then?'

Her spectacles, reflecting the light from the regulation District Council window, glint greyly, masking her eyes.

Connie shifts in her chair, uncertain whether to reply.

A silence.

'You understand, Mrs Munroe,' says Mrs Brown, 'that you'll only be eligible for certain schemes.' She gestures at the map on the wall, pointing to two or three orange areas at the city perimeter.

'But there's – rats – there,' says Connie. 'I couldn't take my kids where there's rats.'

'Rats? On a council estate? Most certainly not, Mrs Munroe. *Not* on a council estate.'

Connie points to an adjacent blue area. 'How about there? I've got friends living there.'

'Dear me, no, you haven't got enough points for that part of town, Mrs Munroe.' Mrs Brown nods her head solemnly up and down as though explaining to a child.

'But it'd be soon, anyway, would it?'

'Difficult to say.' The woman flips the questionnaire over the back of the board, runs her finger down the list underneath. 'You *do* have custody?' she enquires, lifting her head a fraction to measure the response.

'Custody?' says Connie stupidly. 'Oh, of the children? No, no, but I've applied. It takes a bit –'

'Well, until you have at least *interim* custody, Mrs Munroe, there's nothing we can do.' Mrs Brown puts the clipboard heavily down on the desk. 'You see, we're in a very difficult position with you . . . women. Rehousing you. What's to stop you, after all, from getting a better house out of us and then inviting your husband back into it? It wouldn't be the first time, Mrs Munroe, I can tell you. These so-called separations –' She sighs, pushes her glasses firmly back against her nose. 'Well, we've seen for ourselves, Mrs Munroe, time after time you women go back. That's why we like to see interim custody, at the very least. A sign of good faith, you might say.'

98

She leans forward, her hands outstretched in a cajoling gesture. Perhaps she likes me after all? thinks Connie. Perhaps she'll help me? But: 'I implore you, Mrs Munroe, to consider returning to your husband.' Mrs Brown's nose is red with emotion, her hands claw at the air. 'Think what it's like for the children . . . a broken marriage . . . till death us do part, you said, and here you are now running off at the first little upset. Try, Mrs Munroe, try to sort it out. Think of your husband . . . your children –' Her voice hardens as she leans back. 'Otherwise, we'll see you again when your custody's through,' she finishes, reclaiming her clipboard and rising to her feet.

'Yes . . . oh yes,' says Connie, bewildered.

Mrs Brown ushers her out, stands with feet firmly planted in the doorway, scanning her list for the next name. 'Mr Chambers!' she calls sharply. And strides back in.

Somehow Connie has been inveigled into going to Janie's house for a cup of tea. 'Well, being as it's just round the corner,' says Janie, 'and that dreadful old cow's obviously upset you – and – and you'd like to come, wouldn't you, Malc? Just in time to watch the Sooty Show, we'll be.'

'Yes, yes,' cries the traitorous child.

'Well, that's settled then.' Janie takes Connie firmly by the arm and leads her up the stairs and out of the building. 'This way, Connie. Mind yourself on the steps.'

Resigned, Connie holds Malcolm tightly with her free hand and allows herself to be propelled along the street. 'How's Nicola?' asks Janie conversationally.

'Eh?' says Connie. 'Oh, I don't know, really. You don't notice her much. Quiet as a mouse, she is. I suppose we're not being very good about helping her. Carol was always the one for that, making cups of tea, cosy chats. Rose and I don't really know where to start.'

Malcolm is in the gutter, hopping along with one foot on the pavement. She hauls him up, smacks him. Janie winces.

'Well,' she says, 'you'll be seeing her again soon enough.'

'Eh?'

'Carol,' says Janie. 'She's coming back.'

'Heard from her, have you?'

'Indirectly. In the hospital, she is.' Janie sighs. 'Bloody sod broke her arm. Among other things.'

Connie digests this in silence. Then: 'Janie,' she says tentatively, 'I know this is silly of me, but –'

'Oh Connie,' cries Janie, 'I do wish you wouldn't put yourself down like that.'

'Very sorry, I'm sure,' says Connie. She stares away and into a shop window.

'Oh dear, I'm sorry too,' says Janie, flushing. 'What were you going to say?'

'Oh nothing,' says Connie. 'I can't remember.'

No-man's-land.

'Getting a pay rise,' says Jim. 'You come back, you and the kids, and everything'll be like it used to be, like a second honeymoon, Con.'

'Connie!' shouts Janie. 'You don't need him, you don't need anyone except yourself!'

'Mum, Mum!' comes the kids' insistent cry. 'When're we going home? Can we have some sweets? Dad gave us five pee each when we saw him. Daddy says to tell you . . .'

'Remember the sanctity,' insists the woman at the Housing Department. 'Love, honour and obey. A broken home –'

'I want to go home,' thinks Connie unhappily. 'I want to go home where it's warm and safe.'

But where is home? Where is safe?

'Getting a pay rise, Con,' says Jim, his voice far-away and distorted. 'You know what it'll mean –'

'You'll have to speak up, Jim,' says Connie. 'It's a terrible line, I can't hear a –'

'A pay rise!' he bellows. 'In line for another one, too, the boss reckons. Respects me, the boss docs, Con. You want to come back now while I'll still have you.'

'What, Jim?' Connie looks round worriedly for the kids.

'No, really, Con. I mean, fair's fair, you've had your holiday now, and enough's enough. I mean, you should see the dirty washing. And the kitchen, Con. Needs a woman's touch, this place does.'

So he hasn't had anyone else there? Connie, playing with the telephone cord, curling and recurling the white, springy plastic round her fingers, feels girlishly gratified. 'Miss me, Jim, do you?' she says.

'Well of course I miss you, Con. What else've I been saying all this time? And I bet you're missing me, and all, sick of all your lesbie friends, eh?'

'Jim!' says Connie reprovingly. 'I've told you before –'

'Look, Con,' he says, 'this is it, I reckon. You come back now or I'll give up on you. Go and find myself someone else. Pity, mind you, to give up all we've had together.'

'It'd be different now, Jim, would it? None of that . . . none of those arguments?'

'Don't you worry, Con. Keep an eye on you from now on, I will, I can tell you.'

To have his eye on me, thinks Connie. Is that what I want? Yes, I want to be cherished, that's what it's all about. It's all very well for Janie. Protective, that's what he'll be from now on. Protective.

'And you do . . . you do love me, Jim?'

'You just get back here, Con, and I'll show you how much I love you. Right?'

'Right, Jim,' she says.

Later, toiling up the hill to the bus stop, her hands full of carrier bags, the kids running excitedly up ahead, Connie spies Janie coming towards them, tramping over the wet, green grass, her face pink and rosy from the cold. 'Come on, kids,' says Connie. 'Round this corner a minute.'

She watches the other go past.

'We won't have to see her any more, Mum, will we?' says Philip, hopping from foot to foot in obvious jubilation.

'No, Phil,' his Mum says. 'We won't have to see her again.'

But then on the two hundred and seventy-eighth day, hot, clammy, heavily pregnant, sitting on the bus with the three children beside her, she sees Janie through the window, crossing the street, her arm through another woman's, her face animated and glowing. Achingly, Connie watches her weaving her way through the traffic, passing within inches of the window. Janie, she thinks.

'Look, Mum,' says Sharon. 'There's that girl, the one from that place.' She leans across Connie, taps on the window, waves to attract her attention.

'Hush, Sharon,' says Connie, dragging her away. 'You just sit quietly, if you please, and don't go waving at strangers.'

She turns momentarily towards the child, tugging her down in her seat. And when she turns back, Janie has gone.

A WORD FOR IT

Arthur Young

Big Murdie would a wooing go: 'Christ-oh!' said
Murdie.

He still said it. He leant his forehead on the cold glass
at his side and gazed at the dollies in the street:

'Christ-oh! Would ye lookit that! I mean all that arse!
And on the pill and everything! I mean nothing to do
but lay it on its back, end to end, and fuck it! I wisht I
was eighteen again! Christ-oh!'

As he groaned for opportunity not known in his
stalliard youth, his blasphemy sloshed guilt about in the
sludge of my memory. I recalled his impious impudence
and how I had lain awake in a sweat of fear when I dwelt
on it in nights long ago:

'I'll tell you boy –'

He shook his head. It was impossible for him to tell
me how he felt. It always had been. The best he could
ever do was to breathe this audacious irreverence.

But now, the new permissive society stunned him.
The avalanche of fresh female awareness overbore him.

Along every pavement they swayed; on every corner
they swelled out and curved in; at every possible
moment, in every conceivable way those young women
hung it out for display as never before. They knew what
every part was for and used it to the most tantalizing
effect, just level with Murdie's leer. It was so obvious
that they enjoyed their freedom to the last jiggle:

'Christ-oh!' he maundered. 'What I could have done
among that lot!'

I glanced at him quickly: but he seemed about right.

What a truth he spoke though. In his day Murdie was the best nookie man for miles around. Twats came to his hand like trout to a tickle: and his terrible weapon would gut their virginity, leaving chaste entrails in casual shreds; or wound girls of experience with deep satisfaction.

But then, capitulation had been harder to come by. Surrender of that maidenly head carried the awful and ever-present fear of pregnancy: and it could not be slung in a bucket with nine bloody others, all little black eyes, and ears, and feet, and hands and come on Sister, there's four more to do before lunch.

No! The badge of shame had then to be borne and born, all walking, all talking evidence of lustful cuddles: or possibly happed in some kind of respectability by a hasty marriage, with sniggers for a service.

Not that these things deterred Murdie. Indeed risk added spice. French letters were all right, but to get it in bare was the thing.

'Christ-oh!' he would say on the evening of the hunt. 'Nookie-nooks the night, lads!'

'Christ-oh!' he would say after. In his exhalation there was not a hint of the sacrilege which so scared me: more a reverence for some sublimity he had known.

And he would close his chocolate eyes, leaving only the charcoal smudges of his lechery in his white face.

Murdie mumbled. I looked at him again. In the passing lights his brow was bright with sheen. Was he near to vomiting? Had I given him too much?

But he blew out his cheeks and seemed all right.

Whether his mother would let him or no, made no odds to Murdie. She was forever playing whist at the Legion Hall, or gossiping at a neighbour's in curlers and slippers.

But my mother made an odds to me.

You see we were brimstone brethren: faithful for fear of fire. And she was the hottest hand-maiden of her God.

'Oh, Christ!' she would say on her knees in lisle stockings. 'Oh, Christ! Look Thou down on us, fearful sinners that we are! Look Thou into our hearts, our innermost thoughts! Cleanse Thou those imperfections and purify us in thy sight!'

My father concurred in her psalms of expiation, but he was a timid disciple and his tone was plaintive.

As for me, I mumbled to myself in a turmoil of guilt and shame, for Murdie's pastime had shot my imagination with lurid lubricity; and to my dismay his inverted invocation to the Lord not only mocked my mother's piety, it also seemed more genuine.

So when she called on her terrible God to survey my tainted mind, I cringed and could not bear the thought of exposure. And the promise of punishment was incessant.

I strove against sin. I prayed.

But somehow sly thoughts slithered through the barrier and at weekends, half daft with the terror of discovery, I went with Big Murdie on his carnal capers.

I glanced at him again. He had closed his eyes. I took a hand from the wheel, grabbed at his shoulder and shook him violently. I shouted at him:

'C'mon Murdie! Don't fall asleep yet!'

Not yet! Not yet!

For some reason Big Murdie took to me.

Maybe he was sorry for me because of my prayerful parents and their doleful solemnities. Maybe he was evil and needed to subvert my faith. Maybe he wanted company on the walk back from the station, which was a mile from our village.

At any rate he put on a meek face, and his quietest

clothes and asked if I could go with him to the YMCA on Saturday nights. It was in our county town, a train ride away. We could play table tennis and have cups of tea and discussions.

The Christian connotation of those initials, while not strictly strict enough, along with his guileful look and his couple of years' seniority, gave some sort of reassurance to my mother. Although I was force-fed a bucketful of admonitions each time, I was allowed to go with him. I could even stay until the last train home.

Such freedom was frightening. I sopped it up like a dried-out drunk takes his second drink.

On the train journey, Gracie and Muir got in two stations on. They were his shagging pals. Like him they wore zoots and crepe boots. With their shining coifs as careful as any girls' they made a trinity of sybarites who laughed the whole way to town. Their lips smacked, their teeth clashed, and their red, moist throats belled in harmony at the damage they had to do that night, like hounds at a fox's brush.

I looked all eyes. I listened all ears. I put on a string tie, and shoes with sorbo soles, smuggled in deathly stealth. I did what I could with comb and spit.

By the time we got to the Town my prudity was hidden in this new guise: and I got by as their companion if no one looked too hard. Off they would go, me in tow, hunting sure things in the cafes, the close mouths, the dance halls.

Not that I did anything. I was an idiot eunuch; a feart Greek chorus. The thought of talking to a girl, or touching one, was frightening: and as for what they did with such casual confidence –!

So, I got stuck in the corner of a pub with a cider for devilment: or I went to the dance-hall balcony, where I could listen and watch and rock to myself for half price.

But all the time I studied the trio.

I listened to the chat up. I watched the eyeplay. I bit my lip at the bold innuendoes, I squirmed at the slick feels.

Most of all I longed for the knowledge of that soft acquiescence; the melting, until with eyes black with mutual promise, the couples went to get their coats.

'See you at the train!' they would say. Murdie's eye would wink, and I was left to tour the Town on my own.

They usually left an hour before train time. This lent parameters of discipline to their dalliance, for to miss that train meant a long hike, and longest for Murdie. Their evening campaigns were crafted by knowing to a shadow every quiet corner and to a branch every hiding hedge; and by having measured in certain seconds the size of stride and speed of pace needed to reach the station from any quarter.

I was left to wander the Town on my own; left to wonder about these pubic privateers and the prize they hoped to win.

Yet I was not lonely. The red and orange neon signs brought warmth on the coldest night, and the noise of Saturday strangers was always a comfort.

Had we not all come from such encounters: some great, common weal of love? I thought Murdie would understand.

Yet it was difficult to imagine ecstasy in my own conception.

The example of my parents appalled me.

My mother had essayed childbirth but once. To prevent recurrence she indulged in sluicing bathroom rituals with an obscene red pump and nozzle. Its presence on a high shelf with packs of scouring chemicals held my birth, my very existence, to be an unhealthy mistake.

While to my father, begetting me must have been a hurried duty, carried out from the narrow cleft of his long johns which he wore night and day, winter and summer, suiting wool or cotton to the season.

There seemed no way that experience could lead to rapture.

But on Saturday nights, the human race around me told of some rare beatitude. And Big Murdie had no doubts:

'Christ-oh!' he would exult as we walked the station road home.

Murdie rolled his head on the back of the seat and looked at me:

'Need a pee!'

There was a bog ahead. I stopped and went in after him. He washed his boots with concentration, weaving as he stood.

'C'mon, Murdie! Hold up! Not long now!'

Not long! Not long!

I was always at the platform first, eager to share, if vicariously, in their victories.

If one of them strolled up in ample time, eating fish and chips, it had been a bad night: or too easy. To arrive just a few minutes before the train was the hall-mark of a well judged jump.

But there were some whooping nights when an affair was misjudged. There had been unwonted coyness, or unexpected primness.

The careful product of time and distance had to be equated with an untried resultant of likelihood and desire.

On those nights a sprinting young man would be hauled through the door of a carriage already moving. Then he would lie spent with the efforts of his proving, his run and his laughter as he recounted win or loss or near miss. Or there was the odd night when the train would steam away leaving a heaving figure on the bridge shaking his fist at our derision and our disappearing, waving arms.

I listened avidly. I imagined their experiences. But in the quiet places where I worked at my own solutions, there seemed something lacking in the figures of ladies who advertised corsets: and the one picture of a complete nude I did filch had insolent, staring eyes which I thought unbecoming.

'Oh, Christ! Protect Thou us from our base desires! Protect Thou us from the evil in our hearts!'

Would this terrible God never relent? Must this remorseless Lamb be privy to my every waking thought?

It seemed so.

I got him back in the car: five minutes. I looked at him. He would just do.

A new family arrived. They were of our persuasion. They worshipped in the tin Tabernacle with us.

As I knelt beside my mother and father, I came to know their daughter, a girl of my own years.

I came to know her through the movements of her hands as she turned the gold-leafed pages of her bible. I came to know her by the rustle of her clothes as she breathed and made obeisances, heard in supra-sensory sounds above the hymns and denunciations. I came to know her in the indifferent glances with which we sent each other wild messages as our parents talked their way home from worship. And through such knowing a balloon inflated my chest. I thought I would burst.

Daily I dared myself to speak.

I had drawn myself to a tension which must require such release, when I was taken to hospital. It was a matter of swollen glands in my neck, to be treated with patience and rest.

I lay in bed and grew long.

Fortified by months of imaginings, I became resolute. I would declare myself. But when I reached home, she had gone, sent away by her parents in disgrace.

I heard later that she had been able to find a job as a nursemaid.

I pieced the story together with painful care, from chance remarks and cunning questions, making in time a mosaic of misery for my mind.

Oestral fruiting had burst within her with the suddenness of an Arctic flower.

The gelid climate of her religion had not prepared her for the urgings of her germinal humours. She was driven by compulsions which, I guessed, she did not comprehend: nor could her family understand. Neither she nor they had been able to control them.

She put on a display of mating signs. The careful anonymity of our sect gave way to flaunting clothes and colours. The demureness so prized by our elders, changed to a come-hither ogling. But her intent had been marred by lack of tuition and experience. Her attempts were bathetic. She was utterly vulnerable. The terrible rage that threshed within her blazed from her face in the lineaments of a silly simper.

She paraded the main street of our village; defied her parents, and found her way to the Town on Saturdays.

Of course, she was a coconut shy for the lads. They knocked her off, one by one. Gracie in the back of a picture house, Muir in the train home, and Big Murdie on the walk from the station.

They told me with their usual laughter. Why not? I had never hinted about my feelings. I remember my face felt stiff and I had a job not to cry.

It was at that time the fight between Big Murdie's libertine ways and the wrath of my mother's God became too much. My wild imaginings were gelded and my spirit was spayed.

I won a scholarship to the Grammar School in the Town. With relief I settled to a study of integers and graphs. My journeys with Murdie and his friends stopped. In time I took a degree in maths.

In this time, too, I suffered a complete loss of faith.

Murdie mumbled. I said:

'Just about home!'

Just about! Just about!

Big Murdie got caught.

He bairned Famie McPherson in her own pend. He grinned in his pasty face, making the best of it when I met him:

'Just think! I'll be able to lie and soak in it while all you lot have your pricks out for air.'

But even I knew Famie for a fag-end.

After the marriage, they lived in a room and kitchen in Park Street. Murdie seemed to grow down a bit and his face got sharp.

I moved away: and around: then back to my old grammar school in the Town as principal in maths. A lad o' pairts, that was me.

I came across Murdie at a parents' night. I did not recognize the balding man, until he reminded me.

I floundered at my gaffe and hardly took in what he was saying.

His daughter, his only child, sat in one of my classes. A dumb, staring girl, her name had meant nothing to me until Murdie appeared that night.

Her results were bad. Could I help?

I agreed effusively to relieve my embarrassment: and compounded my mistake by suggesting a talk over a drink later.

He agreed with a lift of the lines on his face.

I had sometimes remembered him in envy of my own sterile days. But the ashes of his triumphs were dead in a burned-out marriage.

Famie, I found out, was a nagging disaster: a remould of his own mother, but with bingo and the Eastern Star for her pursuits.

Some remnant of our earlier friendship, some pity for his lost life made me offer another drink. In no time he was maudlin and I was running him home with a promise to meet on Fridays, the night that Famie went off on her jaunts and stayed away until late.

I wheeled him home and with the help of the tongue-tied daughter I poured him into bed.

Afterwards I spoke of her father's request for tuition. She stared at my tie-knot and said:

'I don't know!' in a cow-like moan.

I swore all the way home. What had I let myself in for? Murdie groaned as we stopped.

I wondered again if I had given him too much. He had passed out on the stairs one time, but if I got it right he reached his bed before he fell face down.

I shouldered him from the car. I banged on the door. The daughter now waited in on those nights.

She peered from the open door, frightened and worried:

'Oh! You've overdone it!'

But no! He passed out on the bed. We got his tie and shoes off. We looked at each other in relief. We went downstairs.

And then there was the touching, and the looking, and the loosening of bows and hair. And then before the fire there was the fondling and the feeling with this child of a night's easy ride long ago. And then . . . And then . . .

Christ, oh! but Murdie had the word for it.

A NIGHT OUT AT
THE CLUB HARMONICA

Douglas Dunn

It's that time of night, when hunting cats will be getting up off their cushions. It's that time, when cats will be leaving their pampering indoor premises through half-open windows and ingenious cat flaps. Early arrivals will have already added their luminous watchfulness to the darkness at the top of the wall.

And here I am, being surly at our table, while some somnolent saxophonist improvises on the bandstand; while a half-asleep drummer – dying, I imagine, for a large stiff drink – does his inadequate best to keep up with him, which is more than I can say for the pianist; while a double bass leans like a fat drunk against a wall and its musician has presumably sloped off for a wet or a sandwich.

What is this evening all about? The summer's con-versations feel as if they were spoken a decade ago. I keep telling myself I'm not really here; I'm somewhere else, being nice to people, or reading *Le Savon*, by Francis Ponge. I ought to be in bed, plotting to get my hands on a piece of cake without waking my wife and giving her good reason for directing accusations at the growing circumference of my middle. I really ought to be dreaming.

Young fashionables are being loud at the next table. 'Cosmeticized angels,' I say, 'with damaged wings,' feeling under an obligation to remark on them if only because my companions seem to be observing them with attitudes that look like ambiguous envy. 'Film stars, aristocrats, parasites, and God,' I say. 'These are the few allowed to have a good time.'

My aphorism impresses them like a bad joke. They turn away from the shabby exquisites. I eat an olive. It tastes like a grape injected with petrol.

Fashions appear to have roved backwards again. I can almost hear the sound of far-off propellers and the faint whine of an all-clear. I can see the black market in the waiter's eyes as, eagerly, he obeys my gesture and brings another bottle. Tonight is all about being able to do that sort of thing. I am a colonel of the Free French, with a pocketful of nylon stockings. Tonight, *chérie*, we will have a good time; a little champagne, some cognac, and your legs will never be the same again.

Tonight, too, is about wanting to stick a carnation in one's teeth and take off in a tango. It is about being different from who you are, in the name of enjoying yourself. For some reason, I want to pretend I am a performing seal. I want to flap my flippers in front of my face, balance a ball on my nose, and catch fish in my teeth. If nothing else, I might change the subject of conversation, which tonight is about opportunities in the antique trade.

Oink! Oink!

No salt-stinking haddocks land on our table; instead, the responsibly chilled wine is delivered in an ice bucket by a starched waiter with the eyes of a lion tamer, who looks steadily at me while I look steadily back at him with the eyes of a mouse. Is it time, I ask myself, for my trick with the tablecloth? I make the offer, but the pianist and the rest of the band, refreshed, break into 'Take the "A" Train' like burglars, and not only do we have to listen to this but we have to watch it.

Is this the post-modernist aesthetic about which I have heard so much this year? Two of us decided, on a large bus day in Yorkshire, that the language can no longer be used to describe anything with clarity. 'It is not up to us,' I said then. 'No,' said Charlie. As I looked through the glass of Charlie's new conservatory, I had the distinct sensation of knowing for a fact that his goat, his lawn, the bench under the evergreen, the stalks of last season's Brussels sprouts, the sky, the trees, the stone walls, the moors in the distance – all knew, all *know* where the language is hiding. At one point I felt convinced that Charlie's goat had eaten it. Valedictions all day and every day, but with words like that in it no wonder the language has gone to ground.

A young man, his hair the colour of tadpoles, is putting his tongue into the mouth of a woman old enough to be his mother. 'She's old enough to be his mother,' says someone's girlfriend at our table, excitedly – but is it with amusement or disapproval?

'Perhaps she *is* his mother,' says a friend of mine, and the way he says it makes me glad I didn't get there first. Everyone looks as if words have been stolen from their mouths.

We all look, and imagine we can see family re-semblances. But he gives her three ten-pound notes, so we turn away tittering, except me; mesmerized by the expense, I can't keep my eyes off that rakish young man and his elderly consort. 'There has to be another explanation,' says the girl who started all this. No one else thinks so. Having decided what's going on over there, they are now being urbane. They start arguing about the inflated prices of chinoiserie.

I can hear the sea in the distance, murmuring twaddle about the drowned. By now the band is playing some-thing I suspect they are making up as they go along.

There are sonic booms over Arcadia and Siberia, over northern Canada, the Antarctic, and the mid-oceans, which no one ever hears. There are times when I feel like the ubiquitous decimal in a computer. I want some-one to write 'I LOVE YOU' in lipstick on the back of my white tuxedo. But I haven't got a tuxedo.

Eavesdropping, I can just catch what some bearded little charlatan is saying about his forthcoming *plaquette* of verses. I want to go up to the microphone and announce that Paul Éluard, the twerp's mentor, whom he is supposed to have visited earlier this summer at Vence, has been dead since 1952.

A drunk blonde, singing, is fighting her way to the microphone. How embarrassing for her husband, who is reaching up to hand money to the pianist. Instead of a tipsy discourse on women's underwear in the twentieth century, from the feminist-Presbyterian point of view, which was too much to hope for, she implicates herself with 'Boulevard of Broken Dreams'. I am so determined to applaud this *veritas* that I am applauding already, as if applauding my determination, and she's just started. Yes, I see; I understand why the large party she is with is looking at me like that. She must be popular if her friends, in spite of her inebriated squeaks, think of my stand-up vigorous handclapping as impertinent criticism.

In the gents I want to tell the man standing next to me that the language is sound asleep or dead or that, conceivably, Charlie's goat has eaten it; and that even in remote places the wilderness is dying. But I tell this to the urinal, and bark at the stranger. In return, he strikes me viciously with his fist, straight against the source of my bark. He must have a soft fist – my mouth is not bleeding.

Woodsmoke, cicadas; no, true enough. I'm not here at

all. I am in the *salle d'attente* at the Gare d'Austerlitz on my way towards woodsmoke and cicadas, and it is past 2 a.m. Policemen and ticket inspectors are staring down the beams of their torches. There is the sound of feeble snoring, as down-on-their-luck *voyageurs* wait out the night in an ashtray. No, nowhere in particular. When I reach Corrèze, if I ever do, I suppose the fragrance of the countryside will smell of my disillusionment like that sweaty waiting room, or this night club that tastes of cigars, cigarettes, wine, and everything that's on the menu. When I shut my eyes, I don't know where I am. Trees in the night club, the saxophonist swaying like a deep-sea diver, the drummer carried away on his own furies. Tame owl on my shoulder, what time is it? No, no, I am in the wrong bed, that's not her book under the pillow.

Coupledom. I hold somebody's hand for the sake of appearances. Much has been for the sake of keeping up appearances – fidelity, infidelity, good manners, mass murder. It is the wrong hand. I slap my own hand and pick up another hand from the table. 'What is this,' I ask, 'a séance?' Moonlight is turning to char on the high heather fields five hundred miles away. 'Why are you holding my hand? Give me one good reason why you should, and you can hold my hand,' she says.

'Because,' I say, 'I'm dishonest.'

'And what of your big mouth? Can you keep it shut?'

Discretion, I tell her, is an art in which I have taken several crash courses.

The summer is turning to ice in the head of my friend on my other side. 'I don't feel married,' he confesses. 'I feel undivorced.'

'The grass,' I tell him, 'is brown, black, purple, any shade you like, but it is never green, let alone greener, on the other side of the hill. Grass, friend, is grass.'

'Thank you,' he says. 'You are so helpful.'

'At thirty,' comes a braying voice from the distance of a far table, 'she became something of a bargain, frankly.'

Oink! Oink!

Another bottle in an ice bucket.

' "I let go of life with my gloves on" !'

She tells me to sit down, and I discover that – true enough – I'm standing up. Making the most of this, I explain that I'm playing my favourite game, which I call Hunt the Idiot. She turns away from me. Perhaps she's trying to tell me something. They all tell me to sit down. Seated, I close my eyes, and see things. Lacking the courage to be a performing seal, I could leap up onto the bandstand and make an announcement. 'Ladies and gentlemen! I am thoroughly browned off with the entire universe!' Many people have done that; I am sure of it. They probably survived to live down the humiliation and tell the tale. But what I feel to be absolutely necessary is a gesture that, before these friends of mine, will not be misinterpreted as a cry for help but understood as an insult. In years to come, I will wake up in the middle of the night, chewing the pillow in apocalyptic embarrassment.

That waiter, the one with the eyes of a tout, has selected me as the likeliest source of his tip. The cheek of it! From what evidence has he sized me up as someone cowardly with his generosity? Why me?

Oink! Oink!

'Come and get it!' shouts the mouse to the lion tamer.

Time now, I think, for my trick with the tablecloth.

GOOD FRIDAY

Jessie Kesson

For more than a year, now, you had made a bee-line, first thing, every morning, to the only window that looked down on the outside world.

A vigil shared with Miss Henly, at the opposite side of the window. The lines of demarcation were clearly defined. Neither intruded on the other's vision. Miss Henly spoke seldom. But laughed often. Great gusts of laughter, that caught the ward up in the force of its gale. And left it quivering in the calm of the aftermath.

The turbaned women in the Co-op dairy across from the window were already pulling down the shining levers of their bottling machines. Raising their heads now and again, to gaze across into your world. Waving frantically, when they caught a glimpse of you. The way they might wave to an infant in a pram. Emphasizing their presence.

You never waved back. You weren't a daftie. Acute neurasthenia. That was all that ailed you. It had no symptoms. At least, none you yourself recognized. Except when the passing of time took hold of you like a terror. And hurry clutched at you, like a panic.

'*When?*' You would burst out, the instant the doctor got himself through the ward door. '*When* will I get *out*?'

When becoming timeless. Balanced in the doctor's long, silent calculation.

'*When?*'

'When you stop wringing your hands.'

You weren't even aware that you had been wringing your hands.

The groups of young office girls were making their way through the back gate now. Remembering also. Looking up towards the window.

'Do you see that girl?' Miss Henly's query was directed to nobody in particular. But you responded. Without curiosity. Unable to distinguish the individual, amongst the faces, cast up like foam bells in a whirlpool.

'Do you know her, then?'

'Not in this life,' Miss Henly admitted. 'But I have known her. Somewhere. Sometime.'

That was the summer the swallows deserted you. Silently. Suddenly. As if you had betrayed them. It was *L'Hirondelles* out of a book of poetry the dominie had given you, that lay battened out on the tiles of the Co-op dairy. Basking like kittens in the sun. Secret birds. Exotic. Everybody else thought they were just swallows.

Light as a butterfly, the hand on your arm. But bone and sinew knew the touch of the fragile, tormented partner of your daily walk.

'He's at my neck, again! That man! My poor neck. Nip nip nippin awa!'

'He'll go away soon,' you console. The pain in the hallucinated eyes was real enough. 'He won't come on our walk today!' you insist.

For you yourself got wearied whiles of the third, invisible tormentor, who so often thrust himself on your company. Brief moment of ease, bringing lucid recollection.

'O Jessie. The milk. And cheese. And fine sweet crowdie.'

The young girl, your own age, has taken up her day-long stance by the ward door. Ready to hurl herself on the first man who enters. Whether it is the chief medical superintendent. Or the clock winder.

Madge. Her hand engloved in a yellow duster, is

beginning to weave her way round the ward. Dusting the bed rails. A task unending. Set upon her by Hercules.

All words uttered in Madge's hearing become relevant Essential. Stripped down to ballad bare bones. Only when the ward is wordless does Madge infringe on copyright. And lands you with herself, on Mormon Braes.

> *Where heather grows*
> *Where oft-times I've been cheerie.*

You could avoid such a fate. You could rush to the old gramophone one of the nurses gave you, and put on the two sides of your only record. But usage has blunted it. Time has scarred it, and the heather on Mormon Braes never lost its bloom.

The knitting needles began to click through the ward. The old women, their pale tongues cleaving their chins in their absorption, sat knitting furiously against time. Pink socks for male patients.

Not for you such altruism. The ancient craftswomen, skilled in the cunning art of turning the heel. Could never show you how. Or explain such intricacies.

> *No wise man utters what he inly knows.*
> *Certainty in an uncertain world*
> *Is far too firm a treasure*
> *Wise man goes warily*
> *Jealously guarding*
> *His small particular knowledge*

The nurses either didn't know how. Or hadn't got time. And so your sock had gone far beyond human dimensions, in a year of weaving. Fit only for the seven-leagued legs of some footless giant. Its immensity bewildering the ancient craftswomen. And amusing the nurses.

Penelope? Athene?, aware of the futility of her task, has utterly abandoned it.

The telephone, beginning to ring through the ward, demanded instant concentration. For it never rang, but it rang for you. Even silent. Cradled in its own shining aura of black magic, it never lost potential power. Some day. One day, it would ring for you.

And, although you could never visualize who the caller might be, you stood alert, always. Waiting for the summons. Strangely unprepared for it when it came.

Ginny. Your old china. Linked arm in arm with her new china, Meg. Giggling together at the uniqueness of their surrounding, and at their own temerity. They crowded your small austere room. It was never meant for company. It was the great confessional. Within its dark sleepless hours you made abject acknowledgement of the waste of your days. Strange noises usurped the small room. And crept about it. Shod with caution.

'You dinna *look* different!' Ginny had said, scrutinizing your face. 'You dinna *look* daft!' she had concluded. Almost as if her finding had disappointed her. It was your gear that finally lived up to Ginny's horrific expectations. Your long grey flannel frock. And thick pink knitted stockings. It must have been the sight of the latter that impelled Ginny to urge you to:

'Beat it! Make a run for it! Scarper!'

No fate, it seemed to Ginny, garbed out in her black fishnets, could be worse than having to wear stockings that looked like her 'faither's combinations'.

There were no bars on the window, Ginny noticed. There was nothing to prevent you escaping.

'Dead easy,' Ginny said. Until she tried to raise the window herself!

Convinced at last that she could only leave you to your fate, combinations and all, Ginny had rushed into her next enthusiasm. 'The fella at the gate! The bloke that let us in! Mustard! A real sheik! Was he no, Meg?'

To which fact Meg had giggled her confirmation.

Ginny . . . 'Wadna mind a knockie doon, to him!'

She had insisted. 'You must have seen him, If not, Hen, you must have gone blind. As well as daft!'

Maybe Ginny was right. You had blinded yourself to all the outside workers, encountered on the long, crocodile walks.

They would come back to see you, again, Ginny had vowed. 'Sure we will, Meg. Sure we'll come back!'

Your heart accepted the momentary sincerity of the promise. But your mind knew that if Ginny ever did come back, it would be for another dekko of . . . the fella at the gate.

The ward door clanked open. Jean, massive behind the laundry trolley, pushed it towards the linen cupboard. In every institution in the land, you will find Jean. Hardworking, trustworthy. Too long inside to ever want to go outside. A boon, and a burden to the nurses. Nearly always a burden to her fellow patients. Not that Jean ever considered herself a patient.

Still. It was from Jean that you learned most of the hospital's routine and its precedents. And most of what you had learned was depressing. She always seemed to get some kind of vicarious pleasure from your reactions to her adverse prophecies, which you knew were but the truth.

You would never, according to Jean, get out. You needed to have somebody to sign for you. Be responsible for you, like. That's why she herself had been here for over thirty years. Nobody to sign for her.

Puffing with the importance of having stacked all the laundry away, Jean plumped herself down on the bed nearest the window. She was, she said casually, thinking of having her tea out in the tea room in the grounds. But not until 'they' had passed. The senior doctor and the students were on their rounds. On their way, here. She'd passed them in the north corridor.

The information sent you scurrying from the window to sit down on the bed with Jean. The doctor couldn't see your legs trembling when you sat down.

You might, you confided to Jean, ask the doctor today, if you could get ground parole. And go to the tea room.

'Not a chance!' Jean assured you. 'Not a hope! Because,' she confided in a conspiratorial whisper, 'young girls never get it. With all the bushes. And the gardeners' boys!'

Madge had caught the relevant words, and began stringing them together, in her ballad for the day:

> *With the gardeners' boys!*
> *With the gardeners' boys!*

She had just got it sorted out to her liking, when 'they' unlocked the door. Slipping on her cuffs, Charge Nurse advanced to meet them.

> *In the bushes*
> *With the gardeners' boys*
> *With the gardeners' boys*

At a passing signal from Charge Nurse, a junior removed the songstress to the kitchen. At another, two nurses untangled the young girl who had got herself enmeshed in the group of students. Miss Henly deserted the window, and laughingly pushed her way past the group, and out of focus. Caught unawares, but never unready, Jean leapt from the bed, and advanced to meet the group. Chiding the senior doctor with a familiarity which both horrified and impressed you.

'You haven't been to see me for ages! Doctor Main!'

'Sorry about that, Jean. But . . .'

Charge Nurse cut short the doctor's apologies with a look. And a command.

'There's sluicing to be done, Jean! Have you forgotten?'

'And how are you this morning?'

The other walking patients had disappeared. It was you the doctor was speaking to.

'I'm fine,' you told him. Searching his face as closely as he searched yours. For this, according to Jean, was the doctor who held the keys to outside.

You could feel the sweat gathering at the roots of your hair, and trickling down your face. But you remembered not to wring your hands. And your feet, clamped on the wooden floor, kept your legs from shaking.

'I'm just fine,' you repeated. To make quite sure he had heard the first time. 'Just fine.'

The ward had become itself, again. Each of you took up your self-appointed stances. Friday. You remembered. A good day, Friday. Fish for dinner. And plum duff. Good Friday.

Senior Nurse's weekend off. Freedom. A flush of anticipation all over her. Flicking her cuffs in one hand. Rattling her keys in the other, in an impatience for the clock to strike twelve. Time had truly made you its numbering clock. You could have written out the off-duty lists yourself. But its chimes still startled you.

Rattling her keys aloft, in a final gesture of farewell, Senior Nurse admonished us cheerfully.

'Behave yourselves now, till I get back! Don't do anything I wouldn't do!'

And, uninhibited by the absence of Charge Nurse, her long, black-clad legs skated the whole length of the polished floor. Pausing to chuck Madge under the chin, she turned at the ward door, and bending down on one knee, beseeched of her watchful, wordless audience.

'Why do men adore me?'

And disappeared in a clang of doors. And a flurry of white.

The ward absorbed her disappearance in complete silence. But quivered still, in the aura of her exhilaration.

You began to circle with the bed patients' trays. Madge, beginning to dust the bed rails again, took off once more for Mormon Braes.

> *I'll nae go intae mourning*
> *I'll nae put on my gown of green*
> *For my true love ne'er returning*

Fully in voice now, she ceased dusting. And you ceased circling to join in, and give the ballad the crescendo it deserved.

> *Ye Mormon Braes*
> *Where heather grows*
> *Where oft-times I've been cheerie . . .*

The ward door clanged open. Charge Nurse stood on its threshold. Static. Knowing, no doubt, that the 'artists' – like all *true* artists – could not stop in the middle of a performance, listened until we reached a shaky falsetto close:

> *Fare ye weel ye Mormon Braes*
> *It was there I lost my dearie*

'You!' It was you Charge Nurse spoke to. 'Can get down off Mormon Braes right now! And come and have a bath!'

A bath! At dinner-time! On a Friday!

Saturday was bath night!

'A bath!' Charge Nurse repeated. 'Right now!'

It was only when you got into the bathroom that Charge Nurse told you. 'You're getting out! They're waiting for you round at the front. I didn't want you to know till the last minute! You would have got over-excited. And that would have been that!'

You couldn't be getting *out*. No place to go. No one to go to.

'You're going to your domicile,' Charge Nurse said. 'To the Highlands. The place where you were born. To work on a croft in the hills. It will do more for you than this has done. Besides,' she insisted, 'I never want to see your face here again!'

It was only when you saw your own clothes folded on a chair by the bath, that reality hit you.

'Nurse!' Charge Nurse flung open the bathroom door, and shouted down the ward: 'Nurse! Bring a sheet for this daft lassie to cry into. She's crying here. Because we're letting her *out*!'

FORGETTING
TO MENTION ALLENDE

James Kelman

The milk was bubbling over the sides of the saucepan.
He rushed to the oven, grabbed the handle and held the
pan in the air. The wean was pulling at his trouser-leg,
she gripped the material. For christ sake Audrey, he
tugged her hand away while returning the saucepan to
the oven. The girl went back to sit on the floor, glancing
at him as she turned the pages of her colouring book. He
smiled: Dont go telling mummy about this milk now eh!

She looked at him.

Aye, he said, that's all I need, you to get into a huff.

Her eyes were watering.

Aw christ.

She looked at him.

You're a big girl now, you cant just . . . he paused.
Back at the oven he prepared her drink, lighting a
cigarette in the process, which he placed in an ashtray.
Along with the drink he gave her two digestive biscuits.

When he sat down on the armchair he stared at the
ceiling, half expecting to see it bouncing up and down.
For the past couple of hours somebody had been
playing records at full blast. It was nearly time for the
wean to have her morning kip as well. The same yesterday. He had tried; he had put her down and sat with her,
read part of a story: it was hopeless but, the fucking
music, blasting out. And at least seven out of the past
ten weekdays the same story. He suspected it came from

the flat above. Yet it could be coming from through the wall, or the flat below. It was maybe even coming from the other side of the stair – difficult to tell because of the volume, and the way the walls were, like wafer fucking biscuits. Before flitting to the place he had heard it was a good scheme, the houses designed well, good thick walls and that, they could be having a party next door and you wouldnt know unless they came and invited you in. What a load of rubbish. He stared at the ceiling, wondering whether to go and dig out the culprits, tell them the wean was supposed to be having her mid-morning nap. He definitely had the right to complain, but wasnt going to, not yet; it would be daft antagonizing the neighbours at this stage.

Inhaling deeply he got up and wiped the oven clean with a damp cloth. Normally he liked music, any kind. The problem was it was the same songs being played over and over, all the fucking time the same songs – terrible; pointless trying to read or even watch the midday TV programmes. Maybe he was going to have to get used to it: the sounds to become part of the general hum of the place, like the cars screeching in and out of the street, that ice-cream van which came shrieking I LOVE TO GO A WANDERING ten times a night including Sunday.

A digestive biscuit lay crunched on the carpet by her feet.

Thanks, he said, and bent to lift the pieces. The carpet loves broken biscuits. Daddy loves picking them up as well. Come on . . . he smiled as he picked her up. He carried her into the room. She twisted her head from side to side. It was the music.

I know, he said, I know I know I know, you'll just have to forget about it.

I cant.

You can if you try.

She looked at him. He undressed her to her pants and vest and sat her down in the cot, then walked to the window to draw the curtains. The new wallpaper was fine. He came back and sat on the edge of the double bed, resting his hands on the frame of the cot. Just make stories out of the picture, he told her, indicating the wall. Then he got up, leaned in to kiss her forehead. I'll away ben and let you sleep.

She nodded, shifting her gaze to the wall.

You'll have to try Audrey, otherwise you'll be awful tired at that nursery.

Sitting down on the armchair he lifted the cigarette from the ashtray, and frowned at the ceiling. He exhaled smoke while reaching for last night's *Evening Times*. The tin of paint and associated articles were lying at the point where he had left off yesterday. He should have resumed work by now. He opened the newspaper at the sits. vac. col.

The two other children were both boys, in primaries five and six at the local primary school. They stayed in at dinner-time to eat there but normally one would come home after; and if it happened before one o'clock he could send the wee girl back with him to nursery. But neither liked taking her. Neither did daddy for that matter. It meant saying hello to the woman in charge occasionally. And he always came out of the place feeling like an idiot. An old story. It was exactly the same with the headmistress of the primary school, the headmistress of the last primary school, the last nursery – the way they spoke to him even. Fuck it. He got up to make another coffee.

The music had stopped. It was nearly one o'clock. He rushed through to get the wean.

The nursery took up a separate wing within the building of the primary school; only a five-minute walk from where he lived. Weans everywhere but no sign of his pair. He was looking out for them, to see if they were being included in the games yet. He had no worries about the younger one, it was the eldest who presented the problem. Not a problem really, the boy was fine – just inclined to wander about on his tod, not getting involved with the rest, nor making any attempt to. It wasnt really a problem.

The old man with the twins was approaching the gate from the opposite direction; and he paused there, and called: Nice to see a friendly face! Indicating the two weans he continued, The grandkids, what a pair! No twins in the family then all of a sudden bang, two lots of them. My eldest boy gets one pair then the lassie gets another pair. And you know the worrying thing? The old man grinned: Everything comes in threes! Eh? can you imagine it? three lots of twins! That'd put the cat right among the bloody pigeons!

A nursery assistant was standing within the entrance lobby; once she had collected the children the old man said: Murray's the name, John, John Murray.

Tommy McGoldrick.

They shook hands.

I saw you a couple of days ago, the end of last week . . . went on the old man. I was telling my lassie, makes a change to see a friendly face. All these women and that eh! He laughed, and they continued walking towards the gate. You're no long in the scheme then Tommy?

Naw.

Same with myself, a couple of months just, still feeling my way about. I'm staying with the lassie and that, helping her out. Her man's working down in England temporarily. Good job but, big money. Course he's having to put in the hours, but like I was saying to her, you dont mind working so long as the money's there – though between you and me Tommy there's a few staying about here that look as if a hard day's graft would kill them! Know what I mean? naw, I dont know how they do it; on the broo and that and they can still afford to go out get drunk. Telling you, if you took a walk into that pub down at the shopping centre you'd see half of them were drawing social security. Aye, and you couldnt embarrass them!

They were at the gate. When the old man made as though to continue speaking McGoldrick said, I better be going then.

Right you are Tommy, see you the morrow maybe eh?

Aye, cheerio Mr Murray.

Heh, John, my name's John – I dont believe in the Mr soinso this and the Mr soinso that carry on. What I say is if a man's good enough to talk to then he's good enough to call you by your first name.

He kept a watch for the two boys as he walked back down the road; then detoured to purchase a pie from the local shop, and he put it under the grill to heat up. At 1.20 p.m. he was sitting down with the knife and fork, the bread and butter, the cup of tea, and the letter-box flapped. He had yet to fix up the doorbell.

The eldest was there. Hello da, he said, strolling in.

You no late?

He had walked to the table in the kitchen and sat down there, looking at the pie and stuff. Cold meat and totties we got, he said, the totties were like chewing gum.

What d'you mean chewing gum?

That's what they were like.

Aye well I'd swop you dinners any day of the week . . . He forked a piece of pie into his mouth. What did you get for pudding?

Cake and custard I think.

You think? what d'you mean you think?

The boy yawned and got up from the chair. He walked to the oven and looked at it, then walked to the door: I'm away, he said.

Heh you, you were supposed to be here half an hour ago to take that wean to the nursery.

It wasnt my turn.

Turn? what d'you mean turn? it's no a question of turns.

I took her last.

Aw did you.

Aye.

Well where's your bloody brother then?

I dont know.

Christ . . . He got up and followed him to the door, which could only be locked by turning a handle on the inside, unless a key was used on the outside. As the boy stepped downstairs he called: How you doing up there? that teacher, is she any good?

The boy shrugged.

Ach. He shook his head then shut and locked the door. He poured more tea into the cup. The tin of paint and associated articles. The whole house needed to be done up; wallpaper or paint, his wife didnt care which, just so long as it was new, that it was different from what it had been when they arrived.

He collected the dirty dishes, the breakfast bowls and teaplates from last night's supper. He put the plug in the sink and switched on the hot water tap, shoving his hand under the jet of water to feel the temperature change; it was still a novelty. He swallowed the dregs of the tea, lighted a cigarette, and stacked in the dishes.

A vacuum cleaner started somewhere. Then the music drowned out its noise. He became aware of his feet tapping to the music. Normally he would have liked the songs, dancing music. The wife wouldnt be home till near 6 p.m., tired out; she worked as a cashier in a supermarket, nonstop the whole day. She hardly had the energy for anything. He glanced at the fridge, then checked that he had taken out the meat to defrost. A couple of days ago he had forgotten yet again – egg and chips as usual, the weans delighted of course. The wife just laughed.

He made coffee upon finishing the dishes. But rather than sitting down to drink it he walked to the corner of the room and put the cup down on a dining chair which had old newspaper on its top, to keep it clear of paint splashes. He levered the lid off the tin, stroking the brush across the palm of his hand to check the bristles werent too stiff, then dipped it in and rapidly applied paint to wall. It streaked. He had forgotten to mix the fucking stuff.

Twenty minutes later he was amazed at the area he had covered. That was the thing about painting; you could sit on your arse for most of the day and then scab in for two hours; when the wife came in she'd think you'd been hard at it since breakfast time. He noticed his brushstrokes were shifting periodically to the rhythm of the music. When the letter-box flapped he continued for a moment, then laid the brush carefully on the lid of the tin, on the newspaper covering the chair.

Hi, grinned a well-dressed teenager. Gesturing at his pal he said: We're in your area this morning – this is Ricky, I'm Pete.

Eh, I'm actually doing a bit of painting just now.

We'll only take a moment of your time Mr Mc-Goldrick.

Aye, see I've left the lid off the tin and that.

Yeh, the thing is Mr McGoldrick . . .

His pal was smiling and nodding. They were both holding christian stuff, Mormons probably.

Being honest, said McGoldrick, I dont really . . . I'm an atheist.

O yeh – you mean you dont believe in God?

Naw, no really, I prefer taking a back seat I mean, it's all politics and that, eh, honest, I'll need to get back to the painting.

Yeh, but maybe if you could just spare Ricky and myself one moment of your time Mr McGoldrick, we might have a chat about that. You know it's a big thing to say you dont believe in God I mean how can you know that just to come right out and – hey! it's a big thing – right?

McGoldrick shrugged, he made to close the door.

Yeh, I appreciate you're busy at this time of the day Mr McGoldrick but listen, maybe Ricky and myself can leave some of our literature with you – and you can read through it, go over it I mean, by yourself. We can call back in a day or so, when it's more convenient and we can discuss things with you I mean it seems like a real big thing to me you know the way you can just come right out and say you dont believe in God like that I mean . . . hey! it's a big thing, right?

His pal had sorted out some leaflets and he passed them to McGoldrick.

Thanks, he replied. He shut the door and locked it. He remained there, listening to their footsteps go up the stair. Then he suddenly shook his head. He had forgotten to mention Allende. He always meant to mention Allende to the bastards. Fuck it. He left the leaflets on the small table in the lobby.

The coffee was stone cold as well. He filled the electric kettle. The music blasting; another of these good dancing numbers. Before returning to the paint he lighted a cigarette, stopping off at the bathroom on his way ben.

LINES

Elspeth Davie

As children we were afraid of this woman. Often she was in the park for half the evening, sitting at the bottom of a steep flight of steps leading down into the lake. The park – untended and usually deserted – had once been the small estate of a house fallen to ruin. Long ago it had been pillaged for its stones and lead. Piles of stone blocks and frames of windows filled its courtyard, and in rooms where there was still a wall, tall weeds grew with the birds and trellises of ancient wallpapers.

At that age we had a zest for certain fears. There was the pale young man in red pyjamas who'd stood one night amongst the trees and lamps of the hospital grounds, bent backwards like a hoop to stare at stars behind his head. We feared and admired the strangeness of this pose. It didn't have to be people. It could have been the pit at the unlighted end of town where dead cars had been dumped along with an uneasy heap of tyres that writhed and glistened on windy nights. It could be anything in fact – anything to spike the blandness that our elders had provided to quell irrational fears. Of course we took their comfort thankfully when we needed it. Often however we suspected their version of certain incidents and characters was too smooth, too fluent to be true.

A few years later the woman still came to the park from time to time. But it was different now. The end of school was still a good way off, but it was in sight. We

were beginning to look ahead and we had a lot on our
minds. The ambitious began to brace themselves.
Others grew smooth, in their turn, and listless. The
restless ones got ready to drop from sight as soon as
they left the gates. As to the woman, our fascination in
her had been much reduced. And the fear was non-
existent, though she looked harder than she did in
earlier days – the frown more deeply drawn, the mouth
bitter. By this time we had learnt a few facts to add to the
scraps and rumours of her life.

Long before she came to this part of the country and
while still a young woman she had been for a short time
in prison. It was believed there had been a child's death
in the case, though possibly not her own – and whether
it involved accident, negligence, mania or cruelty was
not known. For some time afterwards she was held in
care. Then she was on her own. This was the trouble.
This was her huge grievance for years to come. She
believed – whether with truth or not – that everyone
now moved away from her as rapidly and in as straight a
line as it was possible to go. At one time she had described
this particular movement to anyone who would listen –
turning on her heel and shooting her arms out in all
directions to show the fearful speed with which they had
gone, as though she were the baleful centre from which
all lines fled off.

Sometimes the woman would be away for a while, but
she always returned to the lake. It was a secluded spot.
Amongst the trees on the slope above the water were
two white marble statues. One was a nymph who had
glanced aside while stooping to wash her foot in a dried-
up bowl. A few yards away was a young huntsman
wearing a fillet of bronze laurel leaves which over the
years had stained his nose and his chin bright green. It
seemed to us that these two beautiful persons looked at

138

one another with anxiety – the girl who tried in vain to wash her greying foot and the youth whose laurels and carefree gesture could never make up for the anguish of green acne. The young boys and girls of our group who came here to meet one another on certain evenings knew all these anxieties themselves, no matter how they were disguised by arguments or scufflings or the great show of scornful indifference which separated us. Yet we didn't come only to see one another. For reasons not clear to us we also came to see the woman. We had mixed feelings. We came from curiosity, from long-kept habit. Sometimes we came as if supporting her in her isolation. Or we came determined to discover by staring at the straight back, where exactly the streak of cruelty might be seen. We'd no doubt that it must be there – though perhaps long hidden – there in the strong hands or the sharp elbow bent back to throw crusts to the water-birds as though aiming darts. Sometimes the forward jerk of her head would bring a loop of hair from under her cap on to her shoulder. As girls who'd never had a covering on our heads we discussed the significance of a bright red beret always worn slightly askew. A sign of one-time elegance?

'But you know, don't you, that the slightest tilt of anything on the head means dissipation?' said Clara who, though the youngest of us, already wore a braid on top of her head smooth as the plaited crust on a white loaf. 'And when I say anything on the head I mean *anything*. Do you remember the first History book they ever gave us? Those tilted crowns on the kings and queens – the wicked ones I mean? It was meant to help you remember the Good from the Bad. And just in case you didn't get the message they made the worst ones cross-eyed as well.'

'No, I don't remember that,' I said.

'Oh yes, of course you must! And some archbishops

were naturals for crooked mitres, and a pope or two of course. I'd never trust the slightest tilt now, not even on a halo.' Poor Clara didn't keep her resolution. She had an unhappy marriage to a man permanently on the tilt with drink and soon began to let her lovely hair fall uncombed to her shoulders as though she'd neither will nor energy to keep it up.

The woman must have known we were all there behind her amongst the trees but she hardly ever looked round. Nowadays her main business was with the various birds of the pond. They literally made tracks for her when she appeared – converging from all sides of the lake and leaving the long, criss-crossing V-lines in their wake. I thought it strange to see the scores of lines approach whenever she lifted her arm, having known of the bitter account she'd given of all those other human lines that had moved away from her during her life. Here the order of things was reversed. Of course she also had the birds in the trees behind, waiting to swoop down when the commotion on the water was over. Sometimes a huge crow landed on the steps and stalked furtively about, ready to make a grab for any bits and pieces that fell from her bag. At the far end of the lake there were always two swans that waited for long enough before joining the squabbling ducks on the other side. Then they would swim languidly across, hardly deigning to bend the neck as they came up to the crusts, or even, at the last minute, ignoring them while instead they turned aside to preen their wings.

One evening however the distant swans turned at once towards the woman when she came down. They took a long time coming over but the lines they drew on the water were as straight and parallel as a double rule. One boy in our crowd – a powerful trouble-maker – happened to be leaning against the marble girl, one foot on the plinth, an arm around her leg. As the swans swam up the woman suddenly turned and raked him and his nymph with an unbelievably scornful and vindictive glance, at the same time managing to look triumphant as though asserting that she could draw this living white sculpture towards her simply by lifting her arm. Though we were used to every look and gesture the woman made, this particular one – aimed directly at him – fairly knocked this boy, Johnson, off his perch. There was something about the look that got him on the raw. It made him mad. In any case he was a spiteful youth known for his bullying way with the younger boys and his knowing sneer for any girl who came near. It was a couple of days later, on a Saturday, that he came down, grinning, through the trees with an armful of toy ducks and swans. Who knows where he got them? He was the kind who would have swiped them from the prams and baths of babies if he'd got the chance. He might have picked them from a counter or from a market stall. They were all sizes including one ugly monster of a duck, for it was the time when shops were beginning to grab on to the idea that Big was Beautiful and very lucrative. This particular bird, he explained, he'd got from his married sister – a discarded, dented duck already supplanted by a bigger.

We were often in the park early at weekends so there was plenty of time for him to launch each bird on to the water before the woman arrived. Silently we watched as each glib swan and lightweight duck floated towards the centre amongst leaves and feathers, bobbing on the ripples that the live birds made. Though we made few distinctions of a moral or aesthetic kind we knew that they were hideously out of place. We would gladly have seen them sink and the boy with them.

But there was worse to come. Johnson stepped back

amongst the trees to collect a large holdall from which
he drew a doll – one of those huge, coquettish dolls
with blonde curls that can be made to represent any
female image from child to adult woman. This one, in
spite of brilliantly painted lips and curled black lashes,
was wearing a baby jacket and frilled skirt. The boy
carried her down carefully to the water's edge, then took
her by her leg and hurled her as far as he could throw.
She landed amongst a circle of plastic ducks and floated
there on her back, her plump elbows bent and her eyes
staring at the sky. We would have been hard put to
describe our feelings as we watched this object. The
girls expressed anger and disgust. Some of the boys
round Johnson laughed and cheered. But not for long.
It was the sense of shame that came uppermost – the
unexpected shame of confronting, out of the blue, the
memory of something we'd once excitedly discussed – a
cruel killing or a drowning, some violent, unspecified
act which had lodged in the mind and which we knew in
our heart of hearts we'd be reluctant to give up.

'That'll show her! That'll give her something to think
about – bloody, fucking murderess!' yelped Johnson,
stamping and swaggering about amongst the trees. He
was not a large boy but he suddenly seemed hefty
enough to take on a prize-fighter – bulging from his
tight trousers as though they'd shrunk to bursting.

Our shame and confusion deepened so much so that
when one of the girls murmured: 'Still the fact remains
. . .' the rest of us drew near to have our consciences
relieved. All except Rachel who at once said,

'What fact?'

'I mean the fact remains that she did – *must* have,
whatever it was – done something black.'

'There was never a fact. It was all hearsay from the
start.'

'Some of it was hearsay. But prison was a fact. Do women go to jail for nothing? No, it's hard to get into prison if you're a woman. They're only too thankful to see you out again. So the crime must have been bad. A child was in it. A child – what else!' We drew back again, each to her tree – ungainly, guilty dryads, preferring never to be released from wood or leaf into the occupations of grown women – mothers or murderesses.

We were all still around this spot when the woman arrived. She came down as usual through the trees looking neither to right nor left, but seeming to show in her face, as she often did, a kind of grim satisfaction in her audience. We watched her as she went out on to the bank and down the steps whose bottom ledge at this time of year was lapped by a weedy, brown water, scummed with layers of autumn flies. She sat down, gathering her skirts from the damp, and made ready to open her bag of bread. She raised her head and her hand stopped on the clasp. There was stillness in the trees as the woman glanced around at the plastic ducks among the rest. We saw her look further. She looked out to where a pink precocious child was floating. The coarse yellow curls had collected stalks and leaves. Over the forehead was a small white duck feather, curled like a débutante's plume. The woman stood up. She turned and began to climb quickly towards us. Just as quickly we moved back to other trees. We'd no doubt we were in danger. Even the bragging Johnson who stood out in the open looked a lot smaller in our eyes. But the woman never looked at us. She was absorbed in the ground, searching intently amongst the stones and rock fragments that lay around. She took her time in picking them up – weighing some in her hand, impatiently discarding others, even giving one or two a little toss to size them up before dropping them in her bag. All this was done with such relentless concentration that we were in two minds whether to stay or run.

'Well, I'm off then! Come on — unless you want your heads bashed in!' said Sylvia who'd had the benefit of a full-grown oak while some of us had a sapling.

'Too late for that,' I said. 'Besides, she's going back. The rocks aren't meant for *us*.' By now the woman was indeed moving down to the water. She let the heavy bag fall on the steps – the crash of stone on marble being somewhat softened by the bread. She bent, took out a stone from the bag and hurled it at a plastic duck. She hurled another and another. She went for each target with such hell-bent aim that not a live duck was touched. Most were unruffled. They swam some little distance towards the centre and waited, gently rocking, their tails to the bank.

The stoning went on faster and harder. Some of the shots came so hard that two or three of the alien ducks disappeared completely underwater, coming up again dented and twisted into peculiar shapes more like small coathangers than birds. The luckier ducks and swans were floating on their sides. Others had let in water and were tilted head-down as though drinking, or bobbing about tail-down, beaks pecking at the sky. The huge, discarded duck from Johnson's sister had died a second death and lay crushed amongst reeds under the bank. No plastic interloper was left intact.

At last there was an interval. It had turned into one of those silent autumn evenings where nothing moves. The marble statues which at first had seemed the only static objects in the park were now only one part of all carved and sculpted things. A wooden woman stood on the steps and a frieze of figures watched behind the trees. I know now it was not only due to a time of year or day. It had mostly to do with waiting. We had been waiting ever since we knew this woman, for one word or sign to confirm for us – once and for all – her innocence or guilt. We imagined this time had come. Out there, maintained in a space between real and unreal, a plastic child was floating.

The woman bent and took a large stone from her bag and with an arm high above her head she hurled it down. It struck its target with a crack and the doll twirled once on the water. Its arms were stretched to the bank. We shrank at the sight. She struck a second time. The yellow head ducked and reappeared slightly askew on its neck. She struck again and the doll jumped. It floated out a short distance and the calm, incurious ducks made way for it.

I remember how we came together gradually from our trees and made our way up towards a stretch of ground a long way from the water. There, our backs to a strip of rusted railings, we sat down – a dozen of us. We formed a council now or perhaps it was a jury. We believed the 'trial' concerned the woman's possible cruelty and the question was whether we had now seen it or not.

'Are you trying to prove some awful past act out of a petty one today?' said one of the girls. 'And there was never a question of battering cat or dog or any other creature, let alone a child.'

'There's always been the talk of drowning, though, amongst all the rest.'

'This drowned thing happens to be a *doll*.'

'The toughness of the woman!' said one of the boys. 'That she could go on pitching stones like that – bloody great rocks!'

Johnson had flung himself full-length on the ground, exhausted by an orgy of vengeance and a race to the top. He had nothing left to say.

As for the rest of us, our muted talk went on for a

while. Now was the time to write her off as human or inhuman – and move on ourselves, as almost adults, peace of mind intact. It didn't happen like that. For one thing various people had reversed the roles and opinions that were expected of them. We were changing. We were divided. Some of us came to the conclusion that there'd been no strong evidence against her at any time, neither in the past nor since. This evening had proved nothing. There was no cruelty in it. Others believed she had been guilty of the greatest crime, that she was a cruel woman and always would be. Clara, the exponent of tilted headgear, had taken up another position, if it could be called that. She was unable to make up her mind. She was not to be questioned. She was not to be bullied. She sat contemplating the lake and its further bank which was gradually turning a deeper blue. Her face looked drawn and shadowed as though maturing rapidly with the ending of the day, and such was the silent droop of her mouth that now and then it was almost possible to guess how she might look in twenty years or so.

It was the woman who made the last move, so to speak. Perhaps she had the last say too, though she didn't open her mouth. It was late and one by one we got to our feet, brushing the leaves and twigs from our legs. As we got up the woman sat down. We turned and began slowly moving towards the place where the ground levelled off into an overgrown drive leading to the main gate. Two or three of us stopped before we reached this place and looked back through a clearing in the trees. The woman was sitting on the steps with her bag beside her. She had used the stones. Now she took out the bread. Slowly, with long, persuasive gestures she began to throw the bits out on to the water. The light was going and the sounds with it, but there was a sheen on the surface of the lake and gradually we saw the long V-lines appear as the black and grey ducks came up. We saw these lines cross and re-cross, more coming from behind – and all converging at the spot where a shower of crusts was falling, to disappear like snow around the gobbling beaks.

There must have been plenty of bread still in the bag but after a time, getting nothing more from her, the ducks drifted off. The woman sat motionless, looking in front of her. We studied her back for the last time before moving on. Given our feelings that afternoon I daresay it struck most of us that we wouldn't want to see much more of her. As a matter of fact we'd seldom seen her face and never exchanged a word. It was her back we'd watched and judged. You could say we were analysts of backs and arms.

It was when the water was almost smooth again that the swans came slowly out from the shadows of the other end – their long tracks cutting the lake like curled-back metal upon metal. They calmly passed the toppled, plastic ducks, the swimming ducks and the submerged doll by the bank. The woman rose to greet them, holding up both hands with the choice crusts. Her back was straight and proud.

BLOOD

Keith Aitchison

It was a sunny week in late August, when the heat curled along the streets and up the tenement stairs of the baker's oven of a city, that Timothy Maguire came to stay with his widowed sister and his nephew.

'By God, have I not brought the good weather with me!' he exclaimed, putting down his suitcase and beaming at them, his round face shining with sweat.

'Mary!' he embraced his sister, then thrust out his hand. 'And this hulking giant cannot be young Martin?'

'I'm nineteen, Uncle Tim.' Martin's hand was gripped.

'Nineteen, is it?' Timothy whistled. 'By God, there's time passed, and a lot of Maguire grown in this lad, Mary. Does he not look like our father when young?'

'He has the eyes, just. The face is his own father's. Come, sit down.'

Timothy sat and pulled out a handkerchief to mop his face and the wet, darkened roots of his fair hair. 'And how is it with you both?' he asked.

'Martin grows up, and I grow older,' said Mary, and plucked at a lock of her hair. 'Do you see the grey?'

'No more than before.'

'That was four years ago. The funeral.'

'Ah, I meant to come sooner. But business, and other things. You should have come to me for a time.'

'I don't think Belfast is the place for holidays now.'

'Maybe not. It's remarkable how you get accustomed to it all, though,' Timothy paused. 'And it's not as if the cause were not just.'

148

'The cause!' Mary shook her head. 'You're the son of your father, right enough.'

'And proud of it,' Timothy smiled. 'Was he not a great man after all?'

'What cause?' Martin interjected, curious.

'You don't know?' Timothy stared in amazement, round eyes in a round face.

'That's enough.' Mary rose sharply, and Timothy thought that right enough the years and the widowing had taken more from her than she deserved to lose.

'What cause?' asked Martin once more. 'Ireland?'

'Ireland! Of course, Ireland,' said Timothy with relief. 'Thank God you've not lost your heritage entirely.'

'Half his heritage, or more likely, remembering mother's opinions, one quarter,' said Mary, going into the scullery and speaking back over her shoulder. 'And remember his father, and his side of the family.'

'Aren't they Irish too, with the name O'Brien?' asked Timothy.

'No one remembers when they came over, but it was long ago. And it's near tea-time.'

'The blood's the same. The years don't change it.'

'Ah, the old blood, who knows who else has got into it over the centuries,' said Mary sourly, 'and bugger the old blood for any argument.'

Martin's jaw dropped at the flaring of his mother's temper. Timothy winked at him and gave a long whistle.

'The language!' he called. 'That's my mother's daughter right enough.'

'Who else would put up with you?' Mary asked back, but her voice was no longer sour.

'Do you remember the time mother lost her temper with that butcher in Foyle Street, the one who sold her the wormy meat?'

They laughed together, good humour restored, and

Timothy went to his suitcase and brought out a bottle of Irish whiskey.

'Just an aperitif, as the French say.' He poured three glasses. 'It's a great pity James is not still with us, he loved a good whiskey.'

'He never refused any whiskey, good or bad,' said Mary, with neither malice nor sadness, turning her head to smile at Martin and show she was not serious.

'Well now, Martin,' Timothy watched approvingly as his nephew swallowed the whiskey. 'I'll be looking to you to show me around Glasgow. I don't know it at all.'

'You'll have an advantage then,' said Mary. 'Most who do know it well have had to forget the half of what they know in order to find out where they are.'

'Redevelopment?'

'That's the name they give it, the smart name so that we won't notice the way they've ruined the city.'

'The progress is a great thing for them as makes money from it.'

Martin listened to them talk, hearing them drift back down the years to their shared memories. The talk, the memories and the unaccustomed whiskey had softened the Glasgow in his mother's voice. The more she spoke, the more an underlying Belfast edge cut through in the words, as if an echo from the past.

'Tell me, how's young Mary and her man?' asked Timothy suddenly. 'Do you hear from them at all?'

'I do. They're both well, down there in Leeds, and I'm to visit in October and see their new house.'

'New house?' Timothy whistled. 'They must be doing well. And you, young Martin, are you going to visit your sister?'

'No,' said Martin. 'I hope to have found work by then, or else I'll still be looking for it.'

After they had eaten, and after Timothy had remarked

that Mary's cooking was still the best east of home, he followed Martin back down the winding stairs and out into the evening, with the tenement shadow sweeping down in a cooling tide along the length of the street, still pleasantly warm for a stroll in shirt-sleeves, with the children calling and playing around the closemouths of the grey tenements curving towards the heart of the city.

Timothy and Martin strolled along the pavement to the main road, and watched the pedestrians and traffic, the city's people in sunlit evening hours between their day and sleep. The doors of the pubs were opened to any cooling breeze, and the sounds of talk and laughter, the clinking of glasses and bottles breathed out on to the pavements in a warm beery invitation.

'When I was in France,' said Timothy, 'the pubs would have tables on the street, where you could sit on evenings like this and take a cool glass. It's a pity we couldn't do that tonight.'

'We haven't the weather for it,' said Martin apologetically. 'It's not like this very often.'

'Still, it would make a great sight, would it not? The Glasgow topers sitting in the rain outside every pub, with their glasses filling up with water and the waiters in mackintoshes and Wellington boots. People would pay to see that.'

Martin laughed, beginning to warm to his uncle's humour.

'And no soldiers,' Timothy mused, watching a group of young men pass by joking among themselves. 'You don't know how lucky you are, Martin. No soldiers, and nobody afraid.'

'I see it on the television,' said Martin, awkward with the sudden change.

'Your television is censored, I'll tell you that. They

don't dare to show you even one half of what the soldiers do, over there.'

Martin shuffled his feet, uncomfortable with this grim note in Timothy.

'Ah well,' Timothy slapped Martin's back. 'Why talk of that now? Your lives aren't touched by it, thank God, and I'm on holiday.'

'And do you see,' he continued, 'how the pubs in this street are positively entreating us to cross their thresholds. Are you a drinking man, now?'

'I take a pint or two,' admitted Martin.

'And two it will be,' said Timothy, and steered his nephew into the nearest pub.

A pint in his fist, Timothy took a long pull and smacked his lips. He looked around the pub with a seasoned eye, noting the long formica bar with plain mirrors behind and the gantries on either side. There were little tables in the corners, and over it all a cloud of cigarette smoke and the hard language of men drinking with no women in the company.

'A man's pub,' Timothy observed. 'You wouldn't be bringing your girlfriends here, Martin?'

'I haven't got one, just now.'

'No? Playing the field, is it?'

'Playing nothing. I've no work, Uncle Tim,' Martin felt ashamed, knowing there was no cause for shame. 'No money, no girlfriend.'

'Just "Tim", eh? I'm your mother's younger brother,' Timothy said, and sighed. 'So, no work and no girl. That's hard. And you'll need the job to get the money to find a girl.'

'I had work. But they laid us off, and it's been the dole for three months.'

'Ah, it's hard. I've been without work myself so I know. I do joinery now, my own boss and it keeps me going.'

Timothy looked around the bar, and the smile returned to his face.

'How do you spend your time?' he asked. 'Do you watch the football?'

'The Celtic.' Martin's chin lifted. 'I go to Parkhead with my mates in the season, when we've got the money. We can't afford the away matches.'

'And tell me, is there that powerful atmosphere we hear about? Songs and the Irish flag waving?'

'Songs and chants,' Martin flushed with the alcohol's gift of enthusiasm. 'When we play Rangers, we do it all specially to annoy the Orangemen. We sing the Soldiers' Song and chant "IRA – all the way!" and all that! It's great!'

'Is it now?' Timothy laughed and emptied his glass. 'Well, that sounds like the sons of Erin to me.'

He stood up to make his way to the bar, counting out money into his hand. Martin started to rise, reaching for the pound notes in his hip pocket.

'I'll get this one.'

'You will not,' Timothy reached out with a work-hardened hand and held him down in his seat. 'These are on me, and no arguments.'

It seemed to Martin as if for once a week passed too quickly. He spent his days and evenings with Timothy. Once they took the train to Edinburgh, together with Mary, and on another day, a glaring hot day, the three of them went down to Largs and passed the day in sunshine on the sand and in the water. That evening, Timothy took them for dinner in a white-fronted restaurant with ropes looped ship-fashion around the balcony rails, and they ate and drank royally at a white-clothed table looking out at the sea and the hills of Arran.

It seemed to Martin that Timothy had lifted him from

the grey drudgery of unemployment, and it was a feeling of gratitude, together with his natural liking for his uncle, that brought them as close and familiar as any friends.

A question of his grandfather began to build in Martin's mind. He had never known him, and somehow the subject had never arisen at home, or perhaps it had been deliberately avoided. As the week passed, with Timothy's presence the vacuum of his mother's Irish family began to fill in patches, like clouds gathering in a clear sky, and subtly altered the way in which Martin saw himself. He remembered Timothy speaking: 'A great man after all,' and curiosity nagged at him with the persistence of toothache, now sharp and demanding, now dull and weak, but always unavoidably claiming his attention, and refusing quiescence.

The night before Timothy left for home, the pair of them travelled to a famously Irish bar on the south side of the city. The evening began to a medley of soft Irish songs played and sung by a blackbrowed accordionist, and later, as the drink flowed both into him and into his audience, and the clouds of cigarette smoke streamed up through the evening to the yellow ceiling, the soft lilts of the Gael gradually made way for the harsher war songs and proud laments of the Fenian men and the IRA. Timothy sang with others in the bar, a mellow baritone in 'Sean South', and even 'The Belfast Brigade', and Martin listened and drank among the other descendants of expatriate Irish, and was swept along on their hazy tides of emotion.

'Tell me about grandfather,' he asked Timothy. 'You said I resemble him.'

Timothy leaned back in his chair and looked at Martin, raising and dropping his eyebrows, crinkling and smoothing his forehead. He sucked the air in through his teeth with a hiss, and expelled it again.

'You don't know,' he said finally. 'Your mother has no regard for him at all; I think she'd be angry if I spoke much of him.'

'Tell me,' Martin's appetite was whetted. 'Tell me! I'll keep quiet, I won't let on anything you say.'

'It's your right to know, maybe,' mused Timothy. 'It's a man's birthright to know the ways of his family. But it's not for me to be telling you. You're your mother's son, not mine.'

'Please!' Martin begged, frantic with drink and curiosity. 'You've got to tell me, can't you see?'

Timothy tapped his glass and listened to the accordionist play a lament for Cathal Brugha. He nodded slowly.

'I will, then. If you don't blab.'

'I won't!'

'It'll be our secret, yes? Between us only?'

'I promise, I promise!' Martin said eagerly.

'Very well,' Timothy spoke quietly, beneath the music's insistent notes. 'Your grandfather, my father, Sean Maguire, fought and died for Ireland. The Brits shot him down on a hillside in Fermanagh, and he lies with the heroes in the Republican plot in Armagh.'

Martin felt the impact of each word, opening and shutting his mouth in amazement. He stared silently at Timothy's serious round face, and knew that this was the truth. His world turned upon itself.

'I never knew,' he managed at last. 'I was never told. Never!'

'Your grandmother had a hard time bringing up us children without a man to provide. She never really forgave father for putting country before family.'

Timothy shrugged, fatalistic at the unchanging strangeness of things.

'You see, Martin,' he continued, 'that's the way women think, that's how they're made. The bitterness rubbed off on Mary, and that's how you never were told at all, I suppose.'

'She should have told me.' Martin said, a trace of anger in his voice.

'It's a secret, mind,' Timothy said sharply, a little alarmed. 'Not a word!'

'I promised,' agreed Martin, and began to fill with more questions.

They drank more than on any other night spent together in a bar. Irish whiskey with every pint, and a pint in every half-hour, downed to the note of the accordion and the singing.

Towards closing time, a small old man in a dark jacket walked among the patrons in the bar, carrying an unmarked collecting can. He stepped up to Timothy and shook the can gently, so that the coins chinked and clashed inside like bullets dropping into a magazine.

'For the boys,' he said with a wink and a grin. 'For the lads and the great cause. Come on now, dig into your pockets.'

Timothy looked benevolently at the small man and winked drunkenly back at him.

'Sure,' he said in his own Belfast voice, quietly, so as not to slur the words. 'Sure, am I not one of the boys myself?'

'Belfast?' The small man asked, stiffening with sudden respect. 'Are you one of the lads in Belfast then?'

'I am,' said Timothy, 'I am, but I'll say nothing more. You understand.'

He reached and gripped the small man's arm.

'Tell nobody,' he gave another drunken conspiratorial wink.

'God's blessing on you, let me shake that hand,' said the small man fervently. 'God keep you safe and strengthen your arm!'

Martin watched and heard all of this, his mouth opening once more in amazement. He was already in an alcoholic fog, and excitement pumped at his heart, catching at his breath. The small man left, and Timothy looked into his empty glass with a little smile.

'Tim,' said Martin in a hushed voice, 'Tim, are you – ?'

'– I'll say nothing,' said Timothy, but smiled fondly at him. 'And you'll say nothing, either. It's the only way, Martin. The only way.'

He left next day, producing like a conjuror a bottle of perfume from his pocket for Mary. Martin he left with a crackling envelope, and a smiling warning to a wagging finger.

'Don't be opening that till I've gone now, you hear?'

He waved back through the taxi window, and was gone. Martin thought that the tenement flat seemed both empty and smaller without Timothy. Even the six crisp five-pound notes in the envelope could not fill an empty chair, and he did not hear his mother when she said with a shaking of the head: 'He's some talker, that Timothy. A great tale-spinner, he could make a living at it.'

There was a change in Martin, it seemed to Mary. He began to go regularly to mass, even to the men's club in the chapel hall on a Friday night, and Mary was pleased to see him taking his religion more seriously. That was her thought, and wrong.

Martin's interest was not religious. It was Ireland that filled his soul, not God. He listened to the Irish priest, Father O'Cahan, and revelled in the soft brogue and gentle country homilies which studded the old man's ceremony. On Friday nights in the club the talk would turn to the old days in Ireland, days that had become rosier and more entrancing as the years sped from them and they sank back into old men's tales of their youth or of their fathers' day.

Martin listened and was no longer only unwillingly unemployed youth. He knew himself to be an exiled child of Ireland, one of the wild geese in a foreign land awaiting the day of return. The older men knew that they would not return, and indeed most had no wish to leave Scotland, but Martin, in the flush of youthful discovery, began to believe that this Ireland of the past lived still, that this Ireland of the cottages and the colleens and the heroes still awaited her exiled children from across the dividing sea.

Martin kept this from his mother, another secret, and a shadow of the secrets he had shared with Timothy. So it was that when the week came which she was to spend in Leeds with her daughter, Mary had no more than the usual mother's doubts as to the wisdom of leaving her son on his own.

She was packed, ready and on the train, and looked again at Martin through the open window of the door.

'Are you sure, you'll be all right?'

'I'll be fine, Mum,' Martin hid his impatience at his mother's solicitude. 'I'm twenty next month. I'll be fine.'

'You've got enough money. Remember the paper money,' she raised her voice as the whistle blew shrill along the platform. 'Don't keep that cold pork after tomorrow.'

She leaned awkwardly through the window and Martin kissed her rouged cheek as the train began to move slowly beneath the high glass and iron roof towards the gleaming rails beyond.

'And don't get up to any mischief!' Mary called back.

'I won't, Mum,' Martin waved and stepped back as the train began to bend away from him along the curve of the rail.

'Goodbye, goodbye!' He called and waved, entirely alone for the first time in his life, already tasting the freedom and the pain.

It rained later, long and heavy, the drops sliding like translucent worms across the windows. Martin lifted his eyes above the grey tenements towards the west.

West Belfast was quiet, the storm-lashing rain driving down the stink of the last night's burnings and tear gas. The army had cleared away the fire-blackened debris of cars and lorries hijacked to barricade and burn, and the streets between the rows of terraced houses were wet and cold, with a litter of broken bricks and glass lying here and there to sign the battlegrounds.

The ink ran in blue smudges down the paper when he looked at the scribbled directions. The rain ran straight down the side of the bag and darkened his jeans where they touched.

Martin clutched his anorak tighter at the throat, and picked his way among the jagged fragments of glass beneath a gable end which proclaimed, in foot-high lettering against a background of orange, white and green: 'BRITS OUT! UP THE REPUBLIC!'

He was almost alone on the streets; only a few hurrying souls besides himself braved the torrent from the skies, but behind windows, shadows behind net curtains or in shadows aside from the direct light through the panes, Martin caught glimpses of the motionless watchers who saw him pass.

Dungarvel Street was on the other side of a sudden ugly wasteland of red ash. Martin started across the emptiness, around pools of dark-stained rainwater and past forlorn banks of struggling weeds. A patrol of eight soldiers came sharply along the terrace on the farther side, and Martin told himself that these were the oppressors of his countrymen, but strangely, the words would not take in his mind, and all he really felt was something like disbelief at the sight of these silent running men, dressed in drab green and brown combat gear, and holding ungainly black rifles across their chests. The last two soldiers watched only to the rear, doubling back behind each other to drop and crouch in doorways. As Martin crossed into Dungarvel Street he looked at their white, dirt-streaked faces and saw, with a quickening of disbelief, that a black and dripping rifle muzzle pointed straight at him, and followed his foot-steps until the corner took him from its sights.

Martin walked briskly down the street, the tremors in his stomach subsiding, but now even more eager to get indoors and out of the rain. He knocked on Timothy's door. No answer. He knocked again, harder. Again no answer, and with mounting frustration, realizing that Timothy must be out working, he stepped back from the door, glancing up and down the street, turning his head so that the eager rain found its way down inside his collar. From the edge of his vision he saw a corner of the curtain twitch in the neighbour window.

He knocked on that door, twice, before he heard a reluctant voice, an old woman's voice from deep within the hallway.

'Who's that?' The words were quiet as if whispered in the hope that they would not be heard.

'I'm Timothy Maguire's nephew, Martin. He's not in the house, do you know where he'll be?'

'His nephew, do you say?' Frail and suspicious words.

'Yes! Do you know where he is?'

'You might be a nephew, but you're not from here.'

'I'm from Glasgow!' Martin almost shouted with frustration. 'His sister's son, Martin O'Brien!'

'Glasgow.' The old voice hesitated, and relented only

a little. 'He'll be working. He's never home before five.'

Martin turned back into the rain and retraced his steps down the street and across the empty waste to a pub he had passed on a corner. Screens of thick wire mesh stretched across the windows like stiff grey nets, with crisp bags and scraps of dirty newspaper caught between the wire and the unwashed glass. The door was narrow and heavy, pitted and scarred like a target.

Inside, the pub was dark, dark and silent, the dim afternoon's light seeping weakly through the windows, and the half-dozen men staring wordlessly at Martin. He pushed back the hood of his anorak, and the rain rolled down his shoulders to the floor, emphasizing the silence with the pattering of the drops breaking upon the floor. The barman raised his eyebrows interrogatively as Martin stepped up to the bar.

'Pint of heavy, please,' Martin put his bag on the floor, and when there were no words in response, he added, 'Terrible wet today.'

'It is,' the barman passed him the full pint glass and held out his hand.

Martin paid, and drank, turning to lean on the bartop. He could see the other men watching him, and he tried a friendly smile and a nod, and the men looked unsmilingly back at him, and then stirred. One, balding and middle-aged in a donkey jacket, walked around Martin and stood at his elbow, between him and the door. Another, younger, perhaps in his late twenties, stroked back his wet black hair and came to lean on the bar in front of Martin, looking him up and down with a thoughtful pursing of his mouth. Martin caught his dark eyes for an instant, and felt uneasy as those eyes slid away across his face and down his length, finally studying the bag at his feet. The young man lifted his head, and looked steadily at Martin.

'Come far?' He had a soft, almost sleepy voice.

'From Glasgow,' Martin replied, then quickly, 'to see my uncle, Timothy Maguire, Donegaterel Street.'

'I thought I recognized the accent. You'll be Scottish, then?'

'I'm Irish by blood. O'Brien. Timothy's my mother's brother.'

'Common enough names, O'Brien and Maguire. But you sound Scottish to me.'

Martin thought he heard a hard edge pushing into the soft voice; a hard edge, a hint of menace, turning towards threat. He could almost feel the man behind staring at him. He began to feel afraid, and swallowed a gulp of beer to steal seconds in which to mask his fear.

'Born and brought up in Glasgow, I suppose I do,' he said at last, and was glad to hear his voice did not tremble.

He lifted his glass and began to drink hastily, to finish and leave. The young man put a hand on his arm.

'Take your time,' he said easily. 'Aren't we just having a wee talk?'

'I'm off to see my uncle.' Martin put down his glass.

'Timothy Maguire? Well, what's a name after all? And this place is thick with the Maguires.'

'What do you mean?' demanded Martin, talking braver than he felt.

'You could pick any name from a 'phone book, could you not?'

'Look,' Martin bent to pick up his bag. 'I'm over to see my uncle, and I'm going now.'

'You're not,' and the young man gave a slight nod.

The balding man gripped Martin by the arms, and the young man casually gripped his right wrist and turned it outwards, so that his fingers loosened on the handle, and let the bag fall. Martin cursed and struggled, and the balding man slammed him hard against the bar, twice, winding him. He gasped for breath, blinking back tears of pain, and watched his belongings being impatiently scattered on to the bartop. Finally, the young man held the bag upside down and shook it, then let it fall to the floor.

'Nothing,' he said, and looked at Martin. 'Not a thing. Maybe it's the truth.'

'Take no chances, Michael,' said the balding man.

'Do I ever?' asked the young man irritably, and turned to the other men. 'Patrick, keep a look-out. Sean, find this Timothy Maguire, and bring him.'

The men left. Michael studied Martin again and jerked his head towards a corner with a small rickety table and two chairs.

'Put him over there, Peter. Back towards the door '

Martin was pushed down sharply into the chair. His ribs ached and he touched them gingerly. He was afraid now, thoroughly afraid.

'What's going on?' he asked, speaking in short gasps, catching at his breath. 'What do you want with me?'

'Indeed,' said Michael, and sat opposite him, 'and that's the whole point – what's going on. This is Ireland. There's a war going on, and you fit the wrong way for us to be happy about you strolling in here and chatting about the weather.'

The barman stuffed Martin's clothes back into the bag, and set it on the bartop.

Michael ticked off his fingers in a casual, unexcited manner, like a teacher making something very plain.

'You're Scottish. You've short hair. You're what – twenty, nineteen?'

'Nineteen,' Martin's mouth trembled and he quickly wiped his hand across it to cover his fear.

'Well, all that means one thing only to me.' Michael leaned forward as if to confide. 'Spy. Soldier. Spy.'

'My name's O'Brien! I'm a Catholic!'

'There's plenty Scottish soldiers with Irish names go to mass. And I don't even know your name is O'Brien, now do I?'

'My uncle will tell you!' Martin said quickly. 'Christ, he's one of the lads himself!'

'One of the lads?' mused Michael. 'A brave freedom fighter is he? Well, well.'

The balding man put a hand on Martin's shoulder and squeezed hard, digging his fingers into the sinews behind the collar bone.

'Do we interrogate him?' he said to Michael.

'You're that eager, Peter,' Michael sighed and sat back in the squeaking wooden chair. 'He could be telling us the truth. Well, part of the truth.'

'In which case we'll know,' said the balding man, 'and there could still be time for the other business.'

He took out a cigarette and lit it, drew deeply and then took the cigarette from his mouth and blew on the coal so that it burned redly. He looked at Michael.

'I don't think so,' said Michael. 'Use it to give yourself cancer instead.'

Peter laughed and drew in a breath of smoke. After a little while he gripped Martin's shoulder once more, and dug his fingers even harder, searching for the pain centres. Martin stood it for a short while, then the hard fingers sent an agonizing spasm through his shoulder and arm. He twisted away and reached up to massage his shoulder.

'Did that hurt?' asked Peter.

'Yes.' Martin felt hatred coming behind the fear.

'Well that's a little indication,' said Peter. 'If you're not what you say you are, that pain will be like a nothing.'

'Leave him alone,' said Michael sharply. 'Violence is a tool, not a pleasure.'

'God, Michael,' Peter grinned maliciously. 'Aren't you becoming the intellectual?'

'You shut up,' said Michael. 'Do you hear me? Shut up!'

Martin listened, and the Ireland of the tales suffocated and died inside him.

Timothy came at last, dressed in his overalls, his face pale and sweating and trying to smile. Michael looked him up and down thoughtfully, as he had earlier inspected Martin.

'Well,' he said finally. 'I know you, Maguire, and you know me. You're no danger to us, or to the enemy. Who's this boy?'

'My nephew, Martin.' Timothy was subdued.

'I'm not sure, Maguire, and I don't take chances. He looks like one of those bloody-minded Scots soldiers to me.'

'He's only a boy!' Timothy took a pace forward.

'I've got boys of his age dying out there,' said Michael evenly, 'and so have the Brits.'

He stood up and walked to stand only a foot away from Timothy, looking levelly into his eyes. Martin saw Timothy turn even paler and look away, down at the floor, shuffling his feet a little.

'Your nephew is under the impression, Maguire, that you're a bold Fenian man, a freedom fighter, one of the lads.'

'Him?' Peter laughed. 'The most he could fight would be a full glass.'

'No, no, a mistake!' Timothy licked his lips. 'I've the greatest respect for you, and I pay my contributions with the best, but I'd never claim your glory for myself! No, never!'

'I should hope you would not,' said Michael, and his eyes did not move from Timothy's face. 'I'm fighting a revolutionary war, and there's enough trouble for us all, without the need to enforce discipline on such as you,'

He put a hand into his inner pocket, and brought out a blue steel revolver. Timothy stiffened, licking his lips again. Martin could almost feel his fear; almost smell his terror. Michael tapped Timothy on the elbow with the revolver barrel.

'You take my meaning?' he asked, and put the gun back in his pocket.

Timothy nodded, making small stuttering noises, blinking rapidly.

'Like I said,' Michael continued, 'I'm fighting a revolutionary war, and you've never even thrown a bloody brick, let alone been on active service!'

'My father died for Ireland!' said Timothy hoarsely.

'Sure,' said Michael with contempt. 'Is that not your style? Another man's deeds again!'

'I'll make it up to you for your trouble, I will!'

'Oh, you will,' agreed Michael. 'You'll be hearing from us. Now, get out, the pair of you.'

Martin stood up, and Peter tossed his bag at him, hard, using both hands, as if throwing a medicine ball.

'You're a lucky boy. Michael's getting soft!'

'Enough of that!' Michael rounded on him. 'Save your criticisms for the proper time, not here!'

He turned back to Timothy and Martin, still standing without moving.

'I said, get out!' And he turned to the bar and unbidden the barman placed a pint in his hand.

Timothy and Martin walked awkwardly down the street, silence between them. The rain had stopped, and grey clouds swept overhead like tattered banners.

'Come on, we'll go up to the house,' said Timothy at last.

'No,' said Martin. 'I don't want to stay, not after that.'

'They won't trouble you again, Martin,' Timothy spread his hands, 'don't judge us by that!'

'Us?' Martin sneered, and stopped walking, to look at his uncle. 'Us? What's this "us"? You've never thrown a brick, remember?'

A car drove past with the slow speed of a hearse, the passenger gazing out the side window at them. Martin wondered what work they were engaged upon.

'If I'd known you were coming!' Timothy pleaded. 'Martin, you must see, you just got in the way.'

'Do you never wonder who else "just got in the way"? Is that how the cause is won?'

'Martin, Martin! You're upset, and I don't blame you. Come on up to the house, at least for the night, and I'll drive you to Larne tomorrow.'

'No, I'm going,' Martin looked up and down the street for the way out of the terraces and back to the railway station.

'Martin, please. Don't let us part like this.'

Martin looked stiffly past, and Timothy sighed and looked down at his shoes and the wet pavement. There was silver creeping into his hair, and a thinning begun at the crown of his head. Martin felt a new emotion: pity.

'Well, just for tonight, then,' he said, and saw Timothy lift his head and smile a growing shadow of his old beaming smile.

That evening, while Timothy cooked, whistling with his jauntiness mostly restored by a large whiskey, Martin looked out the window at the huddled row of terraced houses opposite, on the other side of the twilight street. A puddle caught the light from the window in a lonely splash of illumination, and he thought with longing of tall grey tenements in the rain.

HEART OF GLASS

Alan Spence

Debbie Harry makes me want to cry. Every time I hear
her voice it sends shivers down my back. Makes me feel
happy and sad at the same time. If you can imagine that.
I like everything she sings. Everything. I like 'Dreaming'
and 'Atomic' and 'Sunday Girl' and 'Call Me'. Every
single and every album track. But best of all I like 'Heart
of Glass'. It's absolutely brilliant. Best record ever. *I*
think.

> *Once had a love, thought it was a gas*
> *Soon turned out, had a heart of glass.*

Even my dad likes Debbie. At least he always looks up
from behind his paper if she's on *Top of the Pops*. And
my dad's pretty hard to please when it comes to music.

'There's been nothing since the Beatles,' he says.
'Absolutely nothing.' Then my mum says he's starting
to sound middle-aged and that shuts him up. But at
least my dad thinks Debbie's all right. Thing is though,
he's always calling her Blondie. I keep telling him that's
just the name of the group, but he doesn't listen. In one
ear and out the other. I suppose Blondie's easier to
remember.

The group are good too. Good musicians. But it's
Debbie that makes them great.

The lead guitarist's called Chris Stein. He's Debbie's
boyfriend. Can you imagine that?

Know who I'd like to be more than anybody else in
the world? That's right. I mean, how lucky can you get?

Chris Stein. He's the guy with his arm round her on the cover of 'Eat to the Beat'. He's not even all that good-looking, is he?

Not that I can talk. About being good-looking I mean! I haven't got a girlfriend at all. I know I'm only fourteen. But . . . it's just not that easy.

There's this girl in my class at school. Her name's Moira. She's got blonde hair too. Really nice looking. She's not like Debbie, but she couldn't be, could she? I once got up the courage to ask Moira to dance, at the school disco. They were playing 'Heart of Glass'. It was like being in Heaven. The song and the lights and Moira's soft scent and everything.

Thing is, when the record was finished that was it. I couldn't think of anything brilliant to say. In fact I couldn't think of anything to say at all. I just felt really awkward and stupid.

Moira went back to her seat and the next thing she was up dancing with this big guy from fifth year. He ended up seeing her home.

That's the thing. I mean what chance have you got being fourteen when all the girls your own age are going out with guys of sixteen or seventeen! What are you supposed to do? Go out with a ten-year-old? Get had up for baby-snatching. Fourteen!

I read in this magazine that Debbie is thirty-four. It seems ridiculous. I mean, my *mother* is thirty-four. And I suppose my mother's not bad looking really. For a mother. If you know what I mean. It's just hard to believe she's the same age as Debbie. Thirty-four.

And I'm fourteen, and I wish I wasn't.

Being fourteen is rubbish. Nobody knows what it's like. Nobody remembers. They treat you like a kid and expect you to behave like a grown-up. RUBBISH.

In between
What I find is pleasing and I'm feeling fine
I ome is no confusing there's no peace of mind

You know, my pal Eddie doesn't think Debbie's all that great. But then he hasn't got much taste. He likes Olivia Newton-John for Godsake. He's got a big poster of her up on his wall. From *Grease*. She's all in black leather, trying to look sexy.

I guess I remember her from TV shows when I was a kid. Dancing like a stookie. Singing sweetie-pie duets with Cliff Richard. Pretty disgusting really. So *English*.

Debbie's just in a different class. She's got this *hard* look. Sort of glassy-eyed. Looks like she's in her own world. Doesn't care about *anything*. And yet sometimes you look at her face and she could be sixteen. She's young and old at the same time. I've got a great poster of her. Just a big close-up of her face. Beautiful.

This guy was selling them outside the Apollo the night of the concert at Hogmanay. I couldn't believe it when I heard Blondie were coming. Queued up all night to get a ticket.

I had to go on my own too. Tried to talk Eddie into coming, but he couldn't be bothered. Said it was too expensive and he wasn't all that keen on Blondie anyway. I told you. No taste at all.

The night of the concert I went into town early and spent ages hanging around. New Year coming and everybody getting tanked up already. Big queues outside the licensed grocers. You know that *empty* feeling that sort of hangs about the place. New Year. But all I could think about was that Blondie were in town. Debbie was in Glasgow! I suppose I was hoping I might somehow bump into her. Stupid really. I mean, how could it happen? And if it did, what would I say to her?

'Hello there. How ye doin'? Ah think yer great and ah love all yer records. Especially "Heart of Glass".'

Lost inside. adorable illusion
And I cannot hide

It felt strange, going to the concert on my own. I once went to the pictures on my own. Took an afternoon off school. There were me and three other people in the whole place. Felt really creepy. If you laughed you could hear your own voice ringing out in the dark. Then there was the weird feeling of coming out and finding it was still daylight. The Blondie concert wasn't like that of course. The place was packed. But even though there were hundreds of people, I still felt funny. I still felt *alone*. Waiting for it to start was worse than waiting for Scotland to run on to the park at Hampden.

The atmosphere built up and up. Then the curtain opened and there she was. Debbie, for real, up there in a striped dress and yellow tights, bouncing around in the bright, bright light, singing 'Hanging on the Telephone'.

I had a great seat, four rows from the front. Everybody was really excited. Before I knew what I was doing, I rolled up my Rangers scarf and threw it on to the stage.

And later on the most incredible thing happened. While she was singing 'Pretty Baby', Debbie picked up the scarf. *My* scarf! She wrapped it round herself then threw it into the audience. There was a scramble down at the front and the scarf disappeared. I couldn't get near it. The bouncers would have had me out on my ear if I'd even tried.

Towards the end of the concert the stage lights went down. There was just a kind of strobelight flashing. The keyboards and percussion went into a slow build-up, the introduction I knew so well. I felt tingly all over. Electric. Then the spotlight was on Debbie, dancing to the front of the stage, belting out 'Heart of Glass'. I was nearly in tears.

On the way out of the hall afterwards, I saw Moira. She was with the big guy from fifth year she'd got off with at the disco. They didn't see me, and I think I was glad. He looks a bit like Chris Stein.

The town centre was even more depressing now. The closer it got to New Year, the more folk were roaming about, loud and drunk.

Back home, my dad said he'd seen some of the concert on the TV. He said I should have stayed in and watched it; saved my money. But it's not the same. No atmosphere. Same with football.

'Did ye see her with a Rangers scarf?' I asked.

'Must have missed that bit,' he said.

'Well anyway,' I said. 'It was mine. Ah threw it on the stage.'

'Hope ye don't expect me to buy ye a new one,' said my mother.

By the time the bells were going, the house was full of uncles and aunties and cousins, the people next door, the old wifie downstairs. Happy New Year!

I hate New Year at the best of times, but tonight for some reason it was worse than ever. Before I knew where I was I was crying. My mother saw me before I could get out of the room.

'What's the matter son?' she said.

'Nothing,' I said. 'Nothing.'

How could I tell her it was Debbie, and Moira, and 'Heart of Glass', and my scarf, and not being Chris Stein, and not being grown-up, and not being a kid, and being fourteen, and the stupid New Year, and *everything*.

DADDY RHEAD

Eric Woolston

Right from the day he rode his motorbike up the A55 and bought the disused quarry just at the foot of the mountain, Daddy Rhead was news in the village. He could scarcely have failed to be. Not much more than five feet tall, huge across the shoulders and already at thirty barrel-like round the belly, he had a leonine head that some mistook for mongoloid and hair that he cut with scissors in a straight line round the shoulders after the fashion of a medieval serf. Nobody ever forgot meeting Daddy Rhead.

'Daddy' was his nickname at Upton Comprehensive, where he taught chemistry. He lived alone in the Nissen hut which stood on a mound near the foot of the quarry. At weekends he invited boys from his classes to come over and help him get the place shipshape. They came on the bus from Chester carrying rucksacks and sleeping bags and alighted, laughing and shouting, opposite the Pike-Lees' house with its Bed and Breakfast sign. Sometimes Daddy Rhead gave them lifts up the road on the back of his motorbike. They did not return until Sunday night. During their stay at the quarry they dug vegetable plots, planted potatoes, built a rockery with shrubs and flowers dotted imaginatively round it. In the evenings they sat in the Nissen hut or, if it was warm, round a bonfire in the open, and listened to the stories Daddy Rhead told in his deep but curiously immature voice about his days in the paratroopers.

He claimed to have made over two hundred jumps.

He could remember men whose 'chutes had not opened; men who, in jumping through the hatch in the floor of one of the old-style aircraft had caught their chins on the edge and been killed instantly ('ringing the bell', it was called); men who had fallen into enemy ambushes as they landed. He had an encyclopedic memory, too, for military history; the blunders of Arnhem, Normandy and Singapore, the secrets behind the victories of Rommel, Patton, Robert E. Lee.

But he was not just a talker. The boys could see how he had transformed the old quarry in three months into a bizarre but habitable residence. Some of them had actually watched him driving a hired bulldozer round the site, flattening the ground, removing boulders. He had repaired the Nissen hut that had once been used for keeping the quarry's stores, rewired it, painted it, fitted skylights. Each weekend they watched, gleefully admiring, as some new improvement took place.

The local residents were less enthusiastic. Henry Pike-Lees, the manager of the local branch of the Clwyd Building Society (he had changed his name from Pickles when he won promotion) was particularly worried. He often expressed his anxiety in the saloon bar of the Cross Keys, to which he adjourned on Thursday nights after chairing the weekly meeting of the Conservative Association.

'It isn't just the inconvenience of having streets full of a rabble of schoolchildren – *comprehensive* schoolchildren,' he said. 'There's the noise to think of. People may be disturbed.' Living opposite the bus stop, he himself was often disturbed. 'And then there are – social considerations.'

Henry Pike-Lees was not prepared to discuss these any further but other villagers who stayed on in the saloon bar after he had gone home were less restrained.

'There can't be room for more than eight or ten of them at the most in that hut,' said one of the regular clientele there. 'Not sleeping separately.' He added the last phrase to make his meaning quite clear and a murmur round the room showed that he had succeeded.

Scandalized interest in Daddy Rhead took a new turn late in the summer when a rumour began to circulate about his evening activities in Chester. It seemed that Mrs Griffiths, who kept the village wool shop and went into Chester regularly on business, had seen him on several evenings nipping into a terraced house on the far side of the town. On asking a friend who lived in the neighbourhood, she learned that a young woman lodged there, a flighty-looking piece who wore slit skirts and was something to do with the theatre. After this came out, no further enquiry was necessary. Any respectable villager knew what conclusions to draw. Even so, the new discovery about Rhead did prompt Henry Pike-Lees to admit grudgingly one point in the teacher's favour.

'At least it puts him in the clear as far as the school-boys go,' he said.

Nobody in the pub commented at the time but when he repeated his remark afterwards to his wife, Brenda, she gave one of her jolly laughs. 'May I remind you there are those who can be ambidextrous in these matters,' she said.

After that Henry kept off the subject completely.

With the approach of winter the schoolboys' outings to the quarry stopped and Daddy Rhead began to call at the Cross Keys in the evenings. At first he made his way into the public bar and for a while was something of a success there, telling stories of how racehorses were doped and of attempts that had been made to drug and doctor Olympic athletes. After a while, though, he began to feel that he would like not just to *make* conversation but also to *hear* some, and switched his custom to the saloon bar, where the village's commuters – mainly accountants and lawyers – habitually gathered

For a while he went down well there, too. One evening he went into the question of John F. Kennedy's murder and demolished completely the case against the man supposed to have done it; another time he talked for over an hour about the South African secret police. Yet even while people were listening to him he was aware of a certain reserve, a readiness to try to trip him up if he got some trivial detail wrong or couldn't remember something. Some of the regulars scored laughs at his expense, while others tended to keep their distance, as if repelled by body odour, and then to make satirical references to his stories after they had enjoyed listening to them. Before long Rhead gave up going to the pub. Someone seeing him leave it after his last visit said he looked terribly shaken and spat on the door, swearing violently, after it swung closed behind him. He was seen much less often in the village after that.

The fact was that because of his oddnesses Daddy Rhead was acutely sensitive to ridicule. It angered him all the more because he knew he was as good as anyone. He had seen active service, actually fighting in battles, which was more than any of these smoothies had. He had passed examinations as hard as any that they had taken. Yet wherever he went in civilian life he always seemed to meet with scorn, and ended up avoiding people. As the nights closed in Daddy Rhead began to realize he was intensely lonely.

In Malaya, on the Rhine, there had always been mates. You drilled with them, you trained with them, you jumped with them. They knew you were good at your job. They knew they could end up alongside you in a skirmish or need your help if they broke their ankle in a bad fall. They knew what you were really worth. At college, too, there had been friends; a bit young, maybe, but good for a beercrawl. And there was the climbing club.

But here he could see no prospect of making friends in the village; the superciliousness of people at the local ruled that out. In imagination he said to them, You're a rotten lot of creeps. Well, I'm every bit as good as you are. *And* I can do without you for friends. I'll show you that. By the time the foot of the quarry began to flood with winter rainstorms Rhead had made a new and, for him, extraordinary decision: he had decided to get married.

He glanced round the school staffroom first, but to no purpose; of the women teachers there, most were married and the rest unappealing. For several months he hung about various pubs in Chester in the evenings hoping to meet a nice attractive girl, but none came. He thought of joining clubs, but social clubs and those for tennis, bridge and the like were not him; the nearest climbing club was too far away. The winter dragged on in painful solitude.

His solitude even made him glad of the hitherto rather wearisome duty of visiting his elderly mother, who lived on the far side of Chester. At least his twice-weekly visits brought him company. He had stayed with her, paying a weekly rent to help supplement her pension, when he first came to the district and was looking for a house; and even now that she had another lodger he still gave her part of his pay each week. For a time he had hopes of the new lodger, an assistant stage manager at the town's repertory theatre, but she was usually out until the early hours at her work or, as he later discovered, with her lover. The discovery left him more depressed than if he had never allowed himself to hope.

It was early March when the solution presented itself. In his mother's living room one day, for lack of anything better to do he happened to pick up a pile of out-of-date magazines from on top of her sewing table. The titles were uninspiring: *Woman*, *The Cat Lover's Calendar*, *The North West Post*, *The Church Missionary Gazette*.

The last of them had a picture of Kenyan countryside on the front. Daddy Rhead opened it and flicked through the pages. Photographs of church anniversaries, beaming clergymen, worthy retiring lay workers. Reports of diocesan appeals, proselytization drives in India, conferences on world ecumenicalism. He was about to toss the paper aside when his eye struck the heading, 'Personal'. The column below contained about twenty items but, without conscious choice on his part, Rhead found his eye moving to one item in particular.

Lady, late twenties, (it read) trained nurse, at present working with mission in East Africa, wishes to meet gentleman with outdoor interests, perhaps willing to work in Africa. View friendship/marriage.

Daddy Rhead read the paragraph through, then tore it out of the paper and put it in his pocket. As he did so, he grinned to himself, suddenly happy. Later that week he wrote a letter to the box number given and after posting it he felt a sense of exhilaration he had not had since the army. He rode his motorbike through the village singing loudly, out of tune.

'Marvellous what a girl at the theatre can do for your morale, isn't it?' said Mrs Griffiths to the customer she happened to be serving in the wool shop at the time. 'They say he visits her digs twice a week nowadays.' The two women laughed with a kind of fascinated revulsion.

An answer to Rhead's letter was prompt in coming. It was written in a shapely round hand.

Dear Mr Rhead,

Thank you for replying to my personal ad. I would very much like to make your acquaintance and perhaps I should begin by telling you about myself. I work as a nurse in the Christian Mission here, it is four thousand feet up and very nice country but rather lonely at times. I am in my early thirties (I fibbed a bit in the ad I'm afraid) and love my work here with the children especially. They often have bilharzia from the lake water they swim in. People also suffer from a lot of other complaints and the doctors are always operating on their eyes for glaucoma and cataract. I see you were in Malaya in the Army and so you will know what tropical parts are like. If you would like to correspond so would I, and perhaps we could meet when I have leave in England – or Wales I suppose I should say! (I am from Hampshire so I don't know anything about these foreign parts!)

I hope you will agree to write and shall look forward to hearing from you.

Yours sincerely,

Dorothy Brown

Rhead read the letter five times and folded it neatly into the money belt he wore (he considered purses and wallets effeminate). During the day he read it several more times and grinned to himself. In the days and weeks that followed, his carriage became more perky; he joked more often in the classroom, drawing mirth from the class which, if the truth were told, was more directed *at* him than shared *with* him; but he neither noticed nor cared. He became more independent.

Evenings he would previously have dreaded spending alone he now passed happily enough digging in the garden, rigging up now lighting in fitting a bath (until then he had used the municipal bath-house once a week).

At midsummer he and Dorothy exchanged photographs: Daddy Rhead rejected his first idea of photographing himself for half a crown in the booth outside the chemist's and instead spent a guinea at a studio photographer's. The expense hurt but it was worth it. The photograph was more than presentable, it was even flattering. After that they wrote weekly.

In the autumn Dorothy sent news that she had been allowed home leave for the following summer; she could be in Britain for three months. She wrote about the doctors at the mission, their work, their cricket team (until Rhead told her of his contempt for the game), her parents in Basingstoke, her brother in industry. Daddy chuckled at each letter and put it in a box file with the others. Winter passed into spring.

He was seldom seen in the village now except on emergency shopping expeditions when he had forgotten to buy things in town. On those occasions he avoided the villagers if he could and if he could not, spoke only in curt abrupt phrases. He suspected them all of gossiping and sneering and the deep wound to his self-respect made him brush aside even genuine friendliness if it came from anyone dressed in what he considered a bourgeois or snobby way. When his girl came back from Africa he would just show them.

He liked to imagine Dorothy as rich: in Malaya everyone with a white skin had had a car and Dorothy, though she had never mentioned owning one, clearly used one for her 'safaris'. Daddy Rhead liked the word and chuckled whenever he thought of it. 'That's good, that's the way I like it,' he muttered. Someone in the village overheard him and reported that the ape man mumbled and laughed to himself. The menace he posed to decent people was clearly growing.

It grew again soon after when the news got round that the girl at the theatre had had an abortion. Women began to cross the road, whispering to each other, whenever Daddy Rhead appeared on the footpath. Mothers took stricter care to keep their children off the village street or recreation ground at times when he might be about. It seemed the only sensible thing to do.

It was early May when the bus from the station dropped a visitor with two heavy cases at the end of the village. The young woman saw the convenient Bed and Breakfast sign and knocked on the door. Brenda Pike-Lees showed her to a room.

She was a well-mannered girl, tidy and dressed in homely clothes too light for the Welsh weather. Her physique under the summer dress was somewhat massive, and her face had the easygoing openness of one able to adapt to come what may. She smiled a good deal, as if eager to please.

Brenda Pike-Lees took a liking to her and after dinner invited her to have coffee with herself and Henry in the sitting room. As she filled the cups Brenda began the discreet enquiries she usually made of her visitors.

'You look as if you've come some way,' she said.

The girl smiled. 'Yes. I'm on home leave from my work in East Africa.'

'Africa? Well, well. I expect you'll be touring round to see the beauties of North Wales.'

'Actually,' Dorothy Brown coloured, 'I've come to visit someone.'

'How nice to be footloose and fancy-free.' Brenda surveyed the girl's naive face and podgy build. 'Coming all this way to see a friend in springtime.'

Dorothy did not pursue the subject but sipped her coffee at her window seat just behind the vase of tulips, looking out at the front garden.

'What a lovely village it is. In Africa we have big flowering shrubs but there isn't the delicacy or the variety. This is so nice.'

'Not as nice as it was. It's spoiled by too much traffic and the noise we have to put up with! Don't we, Henry?'

'Yes, dear.'

'For example, at any moment now' – Brenda glanced at her watch – 'A motorbike will tear through here, driven by a long-haired hoodlum, which will make the very walls shake and shatter your eardrums.'

'You always get *someone* like that,' said the girl, smiling, saying the right thing.

'We get more than our share here,' said Brenda. Then, 'Here he comes.'

The motorbike could indeed be heard long before it arrived. The noise was so reverberative that when at last the bike trundled into view it was hard to believe how slowly it was moving. As it roared by, Dorothy and Brenda glimpsed the black-wrapped figure, his hair trapped below the bottom of the face-concealing helmet, gauntlets holding the handlebar in a weightlifter's grip, squat, short and huge. Dorothy half-suppressed a look of excited admiration.

'He's the village oaf,' said Brenda. 'Fortunately, that's about all we see of him. Twice a day is enough.'

'A girl at the theatre in Chester sees a good deal more of him,' said Henry. 'Or did, before she recently lost her figure rather dramatically. It's been the scandal of the neighbourhood for weeks past. Still, it makes a change from the *boys* he has to stay with him.'

Dorothy struck a compromise between genuine amusement and a hesitant sharing of their disapproval.

'No wonder he doesn't let himself be seen much about the village,' she said. 'Where does he live?'

'Up the way. In some sort of hut he's renovated for himself. It must be pretty squalid – like him. They say he was in the army before he came here and he likes to tell stories about it to impress the kids. They always sound like atrocity stories to us.'

Dorothy paused slightly. 'The army?'

'Overseas somewhere. He was actually fighting. Tells tales of butchery, even in his chemistry lessons.'

Brenda Pike-Lees, addressing the room generally in her usual way, did not see Dorothy start or her face go blank.

'Chemistry?'

'He teaches,' explained Henry. 'At the comprehensive school.'

The large girl stopped smiling. 'I expect there are lots of comprehensive schools round here,' she said. 'In an area like this.'

'This one's at Upton. It used to be the grammar school.'

It was a moment before Dorothy Brown spoke.

'And your husband mentioned – boys . . .'

'Oh yes. He has boys to stay *for weekends*. He's a no-good. Somebody one is wise to keep well clear of.'

'Oh.' The girl's lower lip was trembling. 'But he must be independent and – and strong to fend for himself like that.' Then she added, 'Or perhaps his girlfriend – the one you mentioned, at the theatre – perhaps she does a lot of housework for him?'

'I daresay. She certainly does everything else. And now, Miss Brown,' Brenda pushed back her chair, 'If you'll excuse us, Henry has promised to help me finish some baking I was doing. I trust you'll have a good night. Breakfast is at eight.'

As the two women rose, Dorothy kept her eyes directed through the window as if still taking in the view. Before she left Brenda stopped to wipe from off the polished table top a drop of water which the tulips must have let fall, just where Dorothy had been sitting.

The postcard stood on the hall table with the correct sum, two pounds and twelve shillings, just beside it. Brenda Pike-Lees found it when she came down to get the breakfast ready next morning.

Dear Mrs Pike-Lees,

I'm so sorry to have to rush off so early without seeing you but I only just discovered on my stroll last night that there is a suitable bus for me very early so I have gone to catch it. This is what I owe you for bed and breakfast, although I didn't have the breakfast!

Thank you for all the help you gave me.

Yours sincerely,

(Signed)

Dorothy Brown.

It was hardly an hour later that Mrs Griffiths dropped in. Happening to be out early that morning walking the dog, she had seen, she said, a big rather plain girl hurrying towards the bus station in time for the bus that had the morning connection for London. She had been carrying two great cases. Quite apart from the hot-and-bothered look that lugging the cases had given her, she had looked as miserable as sin.

Brenda Pike-Lees laughed loudly when she heard the last phrase. It sounded very apt, she said, especially if a boyfriend was involved.

BIOGRAPHICAL NOTES

KEITH AITCHISON was born in Paisley in 1947. He now lives in Slamannan, Stirlingshire, and works in Glasgow in the Civil Service.

RON BUTLIN was born in Edinburgh, where he now lives and works. He has published two collections of poetry, *Creatures Tamed by Cruelty* (Edinburgh University S.P.B., 1979) and *The Exquisite Instrument* (Salamander Press, 1982).

WILLIAM BOYD was born in Accra, Ghana, in 1952. He was educated at Gordonstoun School and the universities of Glasgow and Oxford. He has written two novels: *A Good Man in Africa* (winner of the 1982 Somerset Maugham Award); *An Ice-Cream War* (nominated for the 1982 Booker Prize) and a collection of short stories, *On the Yankee Station.*

GEORGE MACKAY BROWN has always lived in Orkney. He has published five books of poems, two novels, four short story collections, three books for young people (legends and stories), four books on Orkney, and a play. He has numerous literary projects in varying stages of completion.

ELSPETH DAVIE was born in Ayrshire and went to school in Edinburgh, studied at university and art college and taught painting for several years. She lived for a while in Ireland before returning to Scotland. She has published three novels: *Providings, Creating a Scene, Climbers on a Stair,* and three collections of short stories: *The Spark, The High Tide Talker, The Night of the Funny Hats.* She received Arts Council Awards in 1971 and 1977 and the Katherine Mansfield Short Story Prize in 1978. She is married and has one daughter.

DOUGLAS DUNN comes from Inchinnan. He has published five books of verse, the most recent being *St Kilda's Parliament* (Faber & Faber, 1981) and a long poem with Bloodaxe Books, *Europa's Lover* (1982). His stories have appeared in *Encounter*, *Firebird* (Penguin Books), *Illustrated London News*, *London Magazine*, *The New Yorker* and *Punch*.

GILES GORDON, although born and brought up in Edinburgh, lives in London with his wife and three children. He works as a literary agent, and edits the British Theatre Association's magazine, *Drama*. He has published six novels, three collections of stories, and more pamphlets of poetry than he has energy to count. Last year his anthology with Fred Urquhart, *Modern Scottish Short Stories*, was brought out in paperback by Faber; and his *Modern Short Stories 1940–80* was published as an Everyman paperback.

JAMES KELMAN lives in Glasgow. His first collection of short stories to be published in this country appeared earlier this year, under the title *Not not while the giro* (Polygon Press, Edinburgh).

JESSIE KESSON was born in Inverness in 1916. She has had many plays and features broadcast on radio, and has published three novels: *The White Bird Passes* (Chatto, reprinted Paul Harris), *Glister of Mica* (Chatto, reprinted Paul Harris) and *Where The Apple Ripens* (John Calder).

CARL MACDOUGALL has written for theatre, radio and television. He edited *Words* magazine, was Creative Writing Fellow at Dundee University from 1977–79, received a Scottish Arts Council bursary in 1979 and isn't writing a novel.

EONA MACNICOL was born in Inverness. She has spent part of her life in India where she taught English in a college; and part in a mining village where her husband was parish minister. They now live in Edinburgh and have two sons, one daughter and five grandchildren. Has published historical novels on the life of St Columba (*Colum of Derry* and *Lamp in the Night Winds*) and three collections of short stories set respectively in Loch Ness-side (*The Hallowe'en Hero*), historical Inverness (*The Jail Dancing*) and a Scottish mining village (*A Carver of Coal*).

STEPHANIE MARKMAN is aged thirty-one and has been living in Edinburgh since 1976, currently studying linguistics at Edinburgh University. She has been working in a women's writers' group since 1978. Previously published work includes *Hens in the Hay* (co-author; Stramullion, 1980) and *The Rime of the Ancient Feminist* (Stramullion, 1981), as well as various pieces of work in magazines and anthologies. Her first radio play, *And Then He Kissed Me*, was broadcast on Radio Scotland in November, 1982. She has just started work on a novel.

IAIN CRICHTON SMITH was born on the island of Lewis in 1928. He is a full-time writer, working in both Gaelic and English, and he has published novels, collections of short stories, poems and plays in both languages. His most recent publications in English are: *In the Middle* and *Selected Poems*; *The Hermit and Other Stories*; and *A Field Full of Folk*. His most recent Gaelic work is *An t- Aonaran*. He is married.

ALAN SPENCE is aged thirty-five and was born and raised in Glasgow. He has published a collection of short stories, *Its Colours They Are Fine* (1977), and two books of poems, *ah!* (1975) and *Glasgow Zen* (1981). He has also had plays broadcast on television and performed on stage. He is completing a novel, *The Magic Flute*, and another collection of stories, *Sailmaker*. He and his wife run the Sri Chinmoy Meditation Centre in Edinburgh.

ERIC WOOLSTON was born in Grimsby and educated in Chester. He spent the first decade of his working life in a variety of jobs in London and for the past decade has been a lecturer in Glasgow. He is married with two daughters.

ARTHUR YOUNG is the pen-name of a Scottish family doctor. Educated at Hamilton Academy and Glasgow University, he has published many short stories and, in 1982, his first novel, *The Surgeon's Knot* (Collins).